Miriam Coles Harris

Louie's Last Term at St. Mary's

Miriam Coles Harris

Louie's Last Term at St. Mary's

ISBN/EAN: 9783337107178

Printed in Europe, USA, Canada, Australia, Japan

Cover: Foto ©Andreas Hilbeck / pixelio.de

More available books at **www.hansebooks.com**

CAPITAL NOVELS

UNIFORM WITH THIS VOLUME

And by the same Author.

—o—

LOUIE'S LAST TERM

AT

ST. MARY'S.

BY THE AUTHOR OF

"RUTLEDGE," "THE SUTHERLANDS," "FRANK WARRINGTON," ETC.

NEW YORK:

Carleton, Publisher, 413 Broadway.

MDCCCLXIV.

A

Reverently Affectionate

TRIBUTE

TO THE MEMORY OF THE LATE

RT. REV. GEORGE WASHINGTON DOANE.

PREFACE.

THE author trusts that it is unnecessary to say, this little story is not intended to affect in any manner the character of the very excellent school where the scene is laid.

As regards the narrative itself, it is purely imaginary; the characters, however, have been drawn from life, and it is hoped, are correct and faithful.

CONTENTS.

—

LOUIE'S LAST TERM

AT ST. MARY'S.

—•◦•—

CHAPTER I.

BEGINNING WRONG.

Yet never sleep the sun up; prayer should
  Dawn with the day; there are set awful hours
'Twixt heaven and us; the manna was not good
  After sunrising: far day sullies flowers;
Rise to prevent the sun; sleep doth sins glut,
And heaven's gate opens when the world's is shut.

VAUGHAN.

THE chapel bell had stopped ringing almost five
minutes, when Louie Atterbury, running down the
long corridor, buttoning her sleeves as she went,
paused, frightened, at the door before she dared
open it and enter. Louie was the last; the long
rows of seats were full of girls, the organ had ceased,
Mr. Rogers, in his surplice, was beginning the service, and Louie slipped in through the smallest pos-

7

sible crack in the door, and hurried nervously down
the aisle, looking up very red and awkward, as she
caught the wondering eyes turned upon her.

It was not often that any one was late. These
summer mornings the bell rang at five, and startled
open simultaneously a hundred and sixty pairs of
eyes that had been shut in the very sweetest sort of
sleep during the long hours of darkness, and roused
into murmur the young hive that would not settle
down into perfect quiet again until the return of
night and darkness. It was impossible to sleep
through the ringing of that chapel bell; and even
if the first peal had not waked the girls in Louie's
dormitory, a suggestive shake from Miss Barlow's
not very gentle hand, would have accomplished it;
and having three-quarters of an hour for dressing,
there seemed not much excuse for any one to be
behindhand when the bell rang again. A quarter
of an hour, while the bell was tolling, for their pri-
vate devotions, and then the girls in troops passed
down the stairs and into the chapel. Plainly there
was not much chance for any one to be late; how
did it come, then, that Louie Atterbury was late
again?

She slipped into her seat, stealing a guilty look
at Miss Barlow as she passed in, and confusedly
picked up her Prayer-book and hunted for the

places, doubly embarrassed while she felt her very uncomfortable eyes upon her. She tried, I believe, to attend to the service, and keep from thinking of the reprimand that was awaiting her, but the effort made her knit her brow and look frowning and un-amiable; and it was not altogether ill-temper that made her press her lips so tight together, and bend her little Prayer-book almost double in her nervous hands as she rose from her knees.

Poor Louie! It was the feeling of "everything going wrong," it was the certainty of another mis-begun day, another service unattended to, that was darkening her face so. Everything, indeed, had gone wrong this term. Whether or no the delights of a too happy vacation had spoiled her for the re-straints of school discipline, or whether things were really altered there, she did not know; but certain it was, she seemed to be growing worse instead of better every day, to be getting into more mischief than ever, more out of favor with her teachers, more quarrelsome and unamiable with her com-panions.

"Every one's hand is against me," she thought, bitterly, as she walked out of chapel, "and I can't help it if mine is against every one. Oh! how I hate it all!"

She was too brave a girl to do what she could not

help thinking of for the first minute, which was, to hurry out into the grounds, or somewhere out of sight, so as to escape Miss Barlow for the present. Whatever faults Louie had, and they were many, there was nothing of the "sneak" about her, all the girls acknowledged. So, leaning back against the door that opened into the grounds, she stood resolutely facing the hall, and in the way that Miss Barlow must come from the chapel. Groups of girls hurried past her into the play-grounds, where, in the pleasant sunshine of the June morning, they sauntered in pairs among the trees, or ran wild races along the broad walks.

A few of the more studious had gone direct to the school-room to snatch five minutes of study before breakfast; some lazy ones hung about the steps; the hall was quite deserted, but still Louie did not move.

"Why, how dismal Her Serene Highness looks this morning!" called out Adelaide McFarlane from the bottom of the steps, where she sat idly twisting the heads off the daisies within her reach, and throwing them on Alice Aulay's book, a little girl who had just seated herself there, and who was vainly trying to conquer an alarming array of "map questions," with Julia Alison's help. "How dismal she is! I wonder what made her so late for chapel again this morning? Barlow looked sweet at you, Miss Lou, as you came down the aisle! I suppose you don't mind it, however. You're used to it by this time; and you don't mind going to the Study, either. How many times were you sent there last month, do you happen to remember? I'd like to know, 'just for the sake of science,' how often a girl *can* be sent up and not be expelled."

A very red flush dawned on Louie's face.

"If I didn't mind trying your mean ways of getting out of scrapes, perhaps I shouldn't go so often. Everybody knows Addy McFarlane will keep clear as long as there's any virtue in fibbing, and any other shoulders to put the blame on."

"*Tout doucement!*" cried Addy, with a shrug and a little laugh; "I shan't think of getting out of temper with you, my dear; for nobody minds what a girl says when she's as mad as you are, and as much scared, too. Why, Louie, honestly, *do* you think you'll be sent to the Bishop? Mr. Rogers has lectured you so often, he must be about discouraged."

"If I told you *honestly* what I thought, you wouldn't understand me, I'm afraid. Honesty isn't your native language, you know."

"Listen, Julia Alison, hear how sharp she's getting! Next time I want to write a spicy composi-

tion, I'll do something vicious and get sent to the
Study, in hope of being brightened up by the fright
as she is."

"I'm afraid it wouldn't have much effect upon
you, Addy," said Julia, quietly. "I never saw you
much frightened by anything yet, nor much bene-
fited, for that matter. One would think you might
know better than to hector a girl in that way, when
she's in disgrace."

"Wait till I'm in it!" cried Louie, too angry to
know who were friends and who were foes. "You're
all talking as if I were sent to Mr. Rogers; I am
no worse off than the others just now. And because
you are one of the 'good girls,' Julia, you mustn't
think that gives you license to preach. I, for one,
won't stand it."

"Hear! hear!" exclaimed Addy, delighted. "Julia, you see she's fierce this morning. I wouldn't
trust myself within six feet of her. If I saw Mr.
Rogers, I think I'd recommend a muzzle."

"Oh, dear!" sighed little Alice; "they wont let
me study, Julia."

"No; I see they won't, Ally," said Julia, rising;
"come into the school-room; perhaps we can be
quiet there."

She passed Louie without saying another word or
raising her eyes; but there was something in her

averted head and the low tone in which she had spoken, that made Louie turn away with almost a groan. That was her last friend alienated. Of all the school, Julia's opinion was of the most value to her, and though of late they had been less together than formerly, still there had been no open quarrel, nothing to justify such an unkind speech as this last one of Louie's.

"I know she'll never forget it," thought Louie, miserably. "I would give anything in the world if I had never said it."

Louie was right; it *would* be a long time before Julia would forget the insult. She was proud, prouder, if possible, than Louie; and between two such friends a hopeless wall of coldness and separation is soon built up, from no broader a foundation than this which Louie, in her recklessness and anger, had just laid. Julia was the oldest by a year; the steadiest and the cleverest; and the only wonder was, why she had ever chosen the reckless, self-willed, harum-scarum Louie for her friend. It was not difficult to see why Julia had so attracted Louie, however. Beauty has generally a good deal to do with school *penchants*, and Julia was very pretty, rather small, straight, with a firm, easy step, and a sort of native dignity of manner that "told" vastly among her companions, and attracted while it in-

sensibly awed them.   She was too reserved to have
many intimate friends, and could not be called
popular, but she was universally admired, and as
universally looked up to.   At once diffident and
proud, she only influenced by her example.   This
morning's rebuke to Addy was the nearest approach
to " preaching" that Julia had ever made, and the
cruel taunt it had brought upon her, confirmed her
in her silence and reserve.

What gave this taunt its sting, was the fact that
within the last few weeks, Julia had taken the step
that in the eyes of the more thoughtless of her companions placed her above and separated her from
them, but in her own, made her ten times more
fearful and humble, and ten times more sensitive to
reproach.   She felt most keenly her own unworthi-
ness to be ranked among " the good ;" in her own
heart she was struggling hard to conquer her temptations, and dreaded most of all bringing disgrace
upon the religion she was trying to live by : but
this struggle and this humility only made her out-
wardly colder and quieter ; and her companions,
Louie among the rest, were very quick to set it
down to a feeling of superiority and an aversion to
their society.   This it was that insensibly had
estranged them.   Louie at heart was longing to ask
forgiveness for her constant unkindnesses, and to

beg for advice and help, and to be told whether it would ever be possible for *her* to get into the right path: and Julia, hurt at her coldness and frightened by her growing recklessness and self-will, was yet fonder of her than ever, and yearned to lead her right and to win her to the only means of self-control and happiness; but both waited for the other to speak first, both were too proud to make a single advance.

Addy McFarlane laughed spitefully as she saw the expression of pain that contracted Louie's forehead.

"What a pity," looking slily up at her face, "what a pity that Julia is giving you up! She's such a model, she might have done you no end of good, and kept you straight, for a while, at least."

"You'd better say, what a pity I have given her up," said Louie, quickly. "I hate sanctified superiority, and Julia knows it, and knows that I will not endure her patronizing ways. I can see," she went on, "by the way your eyes glisten, that you mean to tell her every word. You're welcome to; and except that I know she won't believe anything you say, I would tell you what else I think of her, and let you carry that too."

"You'd better take care; you'll be sorry for one or two things you've said this morning," returned

Adelaide, in a tone a shade less trifling than ordinary; but at this moment, Miss Barlow, leaving the
group of teachers with whom she had been talking
at the chapel door, approached them and paused
before Louie.

Of all the moments that could have been chosen
to reprimand her, at least for the purpose of bene-
fiting her, this was the very worst, and perhaps a
more judicious teacher would have perceived it.
But Miss Barlow was too much irritated and too
much prejudiced to see this. She meant to humble
and discipline a refractory pupil; she did not reflect
how far the desire to do it proceeded from a wish to
gratify her own pique, rather than from a desire to
do her duty faithfully toward one of the children
committed to her care. At that moment, any one
familiar with Louie's face could have seen that she
was suffering cruelly from wounded pride, from
mortification and remorse; that there were evil
passions enough roused in her soul already, without
summoning any more to the field, without exasperating her to the obstinacy and insubordination and
disrespect that were certain to follow a reprimand de-
livered at such a time. Besides, Adelaide McFarlane
was her acknowledged enemy and tormentor, and .
sat by now, with greedy eyes, watching the encounter, and her presence, of course, was an irritation.

I do not mean to make any excuses for Louie; there is no need for me to hold up her faults for execration; they punished themselves every step she took; no one could fail to see how miserable she was, and there is no danger of her having any followers, merely for the pleasure her career promised. What I wish to do is to be just; to show how many influences were at work to lead her so far astray. I do not wish wholly to blame Miss Barlow; she meant well, and in the main did her duty as a teacher; but toward this girl she had allowed herself to be too easily prejudiced, and had not taken the pains to sift her feelings and inquire into their justice. . Miss Barlow had not brought her own temper under entire control, so it is not to be wondered at that she failed to control her pupil; and when she paused in front of her, there was an angry gleam from her black eye, and an excited tremor in her voice, that certainly were not calculated to soothe a ruffled temper, or to insure complete submission.

"How do you explain your tardiness again this morning, Louisa?" There was a moment's pause; Louie tried to answer, but the words choked her. She was literally too much worked up to command her voice.

"Do you mean to answer me?" demanded the teacher in a sharper tone.

Louie caught a glance of Adelaide's eager eye; she gave a sort of gasp and said quickly:

"I have no explanation to give."

"Think again before you make that decisive; it will be worse for you than you imagine if you continue to rebel."

"It can't be worse for me than it has been for the last month," muttered Louie under her breath.

"Once for all," said Miss Barlow in a tone of suppressed anger, and looking steadily at her, "do you mean to explain to me the circumstance of your tardiness this morning?"

"I do not."

There was the deadest silence; Adelaide held her breath with excitement, the teacher with anger; Louie alone was composed enough now. All the wavering and timidity was gone, she had not a thought that was not hatred and rebellion.

"Go to the Study at once," was all that Miss Barlow could find voice to say, as she motioned her away.

Louie bowed slightly as she left her, and with a very firm step walked across the hall, and entered the Study door.

CHAPTER II.

THE STUDY.

"Anger's a hurricane inbred;
  Meekness, a calm in heart and head;
  Revenge, of war runs all the ills;
  Forgiveness, sweets of peace instills."

BISHOP KEN.

THE precise nature of the punishment implied in the sentence of banishment to the Study, may possibly need explanation to those whose misfortune it has been not to have been educated at St. Mary's Hall. When I confess that its terrors were more imaginary than substantial, it will be understood that I look back at it from some distance of time, and with the disenchantment of several years between it and me. During the entire period of my school career, however, I stood in a very salutary awe of its thunders, and regarded the sentence with all the dread that it was meant to inspire.

In plain fact, the Study was a very large and commodious room, somewhat dark, perhaps, and not altogether cheerful, filled with bookcases and

books, and having a very learned look withal, pre-
sided over by the Chaplain of the Hall, in my time
a most humane and kind gentleman, and one
against whom an act of severity or injustice had
never been recorded. He was very ready to excuse youthful faults, and decreed for all ordinary
offences, very mild and bearable punishments, re-
ferring the extremest cases to the Bishop's decision.
The result of being sent to the Study, in fine, was,
generally, fifteen minutes' interview with this
gentleman, a good deal of good advice, a little kind
expostulation on the impropriety of the fault for
which the offender was arraigned, a recommenda-
tion to the mercy of the Principal, and a "good
morning."

Notwithstanding this known result, being sent to
the Study was always a horrible and disgraceful
thing; the stoutest hearts quaked a little at it; it
threw the timid ones into an agony of alarm and
apprehension, and all agreed to look with some pity
and much contempt upon the unhappy subjects of
the decree. Thus it was, that as Louie Atterbury
walked across the hall toward the Study door, she
heard with some concern the ringing of the break-
fast-bell, and the rush of feet that followed it in-
stantly. She was too proud to hurry; the foremost
ones caught sight of her, and too proud to shut the

Study door after her, so the bolder ones, hearing the rumor of her disgrace, stole on tip-toe half across the hall and peeped in at her. She had seated herself on a chair by the window, and when she saw the prying faces of her tormentors, she bit her lip; but, forcing back the tears, gave them a careless nod and smile.

Mr. Rogers, passing that moment on his way to breakfast, looked in upon her; he saw the nod and smile, and his face darkened. No one in authority, however kind, can endure to see his authority mocked at and derided.

"You may wait here till I come back," he said, coldly.

Louie listened to the tramp of feet down the dining-room stairs; how long before it ceased! then the pause while grace was said; then the sudden noise of the adjustment and occupation of all that multitude of chairs, and soon the subdued sounds of knife and fork as the besieging army of hungry girls applied themselves to their repast. Louie thought of the inquiring eyes that would be turned toward her empty place.

"There isn't a soul in school that won't know I'm sent to the Study, before ten minutes are over," she thought, dismally, "and, moreover, that it's the second time this month. A pretty sort of name

I'm getting! Well, I can't help it; I don't care."

And she pressed her lips tighter together, and, leaning back in her chair, beat uneasily with her foot upon the carpet, and muttered again with a darkened brow, "I don't care."

Poor Louie! If she hadn't cared, she would never have worn such a face as she wore then; she wouldn't have bit her pale lips so, nor have beaten that nervous tatto upon the carpet. She did care, and bitterly, too, about the bad name she was getting; but she did not care in the right sort of a way, nor try the right sort of means to prevent it. Pride and self-will had brought it upon her, and by pride and self-will she was trying (as far as she tried at all) to get rid of it. Alice Aulay, eight years old, could have told her that that was not the way; any girl in the school could have told her that two wrongs didn't make a right; her own heart, if she had listened to it, could have told her that humility and self-denial were the opposites of pride and self-will; and that only by renouncing these and assuming those, could she attain to the favor of God and man.

But she didn't listen to it. She went blindly, blunderingly, obstinately on, listening to the tumult of evil thoughts that beset her—to the evil suggestions of her companions and the evil suggestions of the devil, and the faint voice of conscience was stifled before it reached her ear. Sometimes, in the hush of the Chapel service, or when she saw her young companions kneel around the altar that she hardly dared look upon, there would come a memory of her baptismal blessings—a thought of what she had been made, and what she ought even now to be; but a bitter sigh would blot it all out.

"I need not try to be good. I have tried and failed so often. I cannot go with Julia and the others. I am growing worse instead of better. I must be, oh, how different before I am fit for the Communion! It will be long, if ever, before I am good enough to go; but it is not my fault. I cannot help it if I am wicked; I cannot help it if I am worse than they are."

And so, trying to satisfy herself that it was not her fault, she went on in the wrong ways that had been thickening round her of late, unsatisfied and very miserable, but very unrepentant.

When Mr. Rogers, accompanied by Miss Barlow, entered the Study half an hour later, they found as unhopeful a subject in it as they had left. If Mr. Rogers had been alone, Louie had made up her mind to be submissive, and apologize and tell him all he desired to know; but when the door opened and his grave face appeared, preceded by

the face that was associated in her mind with all
the stormy scenes she had gone through in the last
year, the good resolution, founded as it was in only
another form of self-will, faded quickly, and a stubborn rebellion took possession of her. All Mr.
Rogers' kindness was forgotten in the recollection
of Miss Barlow's injustice; she could see nothing
but tyranny, feel nothing but defiance.

I think Miss Barlow comprehended this at a
glance, for her thin lip curled slightly, and her
sharp eye emitted an angry light. "I fear you will
have to resort to harsher measures, Mr. Rogers,"
she said in a low tone.

"Harsh measures are very disagreeable to me,"
he answered aloud, "and I shall not willingly
have recourse to them; but I suppose there is no
girl in this school so ignorant of right and justice
as to suppose that rebellion to lawful authority will
be tolerated in it. Kindness and indulgence must
have a limit, or they are abused."

"Yes, sir," said Louie, quickly, "and prejudice
and persecution must have a limit, or *they* are
abused."

The blood started to Miss Barlow's cheek, and
she looked from Louie to the clergyman as if to
say, "You see, sir, it is as I said."

Mr. Rogers did not regard the glance, but continued to look sternly at the girl, sternly but thoughtfully.

"You cannot doubt but that I am as ready to put down persecution and oppression, as to punish . disrespect and insubordination. You have been accused more than once of the last, and you know it forms the present charge against you. Let us settle that matter first, and then whatever complaints you have to make of injustice and persecution, I am ready to hear and to endeavor to redress. Now for the question in hand.

"You are aware, Louisa, that this is by no means the first time that I have had complaints brought me of you. I have always treated you with the greatest consideration and kindness when I have been obliged to reprimand you, hoping by that means to win you to a wiser course. Those measures, I see, have entirely failed, and I must try another method with you. Now, I wish you distinctly to understand, before we go any further, that I mean to establish Miss Barlow's authority, and that obedience to her is to be all that will save you from severity. She tells me that you have refused to answer her questions in regard to a breach of rules this morning. The fewer words we waste now the better: I ask you, therefore, do you continue to refuse an explanation to her?"

2

Louie glanced an instant at Miss Barlow, and her resolution was fixed.

"I will explain it to you, sir. I will not explain it to Miss Barlow."

There was a pair of very angry, and a pair of very stern eyes bent on the girl for several minutes after she said this, but she did not tremble nor falter, though she heard in a sort of bewildered dream the words that followed. She hardly understood their import, though she mechanically obeyed them, leaving the room and going up to her dormitory where she was to stay through the day. Mr. Rogers' last sentence as she left the study, sounded in her ears:

"I give you till to-morrow morning to think it over. By that time I trust you will have concluded to obey me, and to submit to the authority of your teacher."

"I will die first!" muttered Louie between her teeth as she shut the dormitory door firmly, and walked through the long empty room to her own bed which stood beside the window at the extreme end. "I will die before I submit to her! Let them expel me, if they please. I don't care much what they do to me, nor what becomes of me. As well be expelled as stay here, where nobody respects me, and nobody thinks of loving me!"

She leaned against the window and looked out. The light fell flickeringly on the grassy bank through the waving branches of the great trees before the house, and the river gleamed bright and blue in the sunshine. The soft June wind, sweet with neighboring flowers, blew in at the open window, and stirred the leaves of Louie's little Bible lying on the sill. She glanced down at it a moment, and her eye fell on the words written on the blank leaf, fluttering now in the wind,

"LOUIE ATTERBURY, FROM HER MOTHER."

A blinding mist of tears came between her and the words. "What would mother say if she knew of this! and little Larry, who thinks I am so good!"

And choking with sobs, she threw herself upon the bed and buried her face in the pillow. But there was no danger that her mother would know of her disgrace; no danger and no hope either. Thousands of miles of ocean rolled between her and her child, and Louie's trial would be many weeks old before her mother could hear of it, would have settled her in sin or brought her to repentance before her mother could, by counsel or entreaty, help her to see the right. She was beyond the reach of anything but her mother's prayers now, poor girl, but she had sore need of them.

It had been, indeed, almost like death, the parting a year before between Louie and her mother.
A child more petted and indulged, more necessary
to a parent, more companionable and devoted, had
never lived.   Cruel as the separation was to Louie,
no doubt it came harder to the mother, for besides
the pain of living without her, there were heavy
fears for the effect it might have upon her child.
These were the most dangerous years of her life,
and Louie was a child to love with a pain at your
heart, a love compounded of foreboding and yearning and tenderness was the love that she inspired.
The very qualities that made you love her, created
a dread as well.

But a stronger duty than her child's guidance,
even, called the mother away.   Captain Atterbury
had been ordered to the coast of the Mediterranean,
and there was no question about her duty in following him.   She had taken Larry, her little son, with
her, leaving Louie at the school in which she had
the most confidence, with many pangs to be sure,
but with an entire faith that, as she had done as
nearly right as she knew, all would go on right.
But for several months Louie had taken it dreadfully
to heart.   She had been, *par excellence* " the homesick girl" of the school, had moped and pined till
those who had the care of her had really feared for

her health. At last, however, her natural spirits and the kindness and consideration of those around her, won her back to her ordinary lightheartedness and vivacity; and the direful homesickness and depression of the first separation only occasionally returned—sometimes, when the long-looked-for letters revived it for the moment by their tenderness, or when the harshness of any of those about her, or some fit of self-reproach, brought to her mind too vividly the care and companionship she had lost.

"Oh! if I could be with mother I should not be so bad, I know! I know I should be good!" she sobbed, as she lay face downward on the bed. The tears did her good; they carried away half the stubbornness in her heart. I don't know how long she laid there, sobbing as she thought of her mother's goodness and her own wickedness, resolving and re-resolving that indeed she would be better; before, exhausted with excitement and faint for want of food, she yielded to the sleep that came over her, and dreamed sweet dreams of mother and Larry, and forgot school and trouble as much as if she had indeed been with them in their pleasant Italian home.

Her sleep was long and heavy, even the Chapel bell at noon did not wake her, nor the opening of the door just after, and the cautious entrance of Adelaide McFarlane into the room. Her bed was next but one to Louie's, and she stole quietly along to it, looking with wonder and a sort of malice at the quiet sleeper. Addy's eyes were very light blue, and they ordinarily had but a faint expression of anything in them; but on this occasion they gleamed with some very decided feeling. Hatred, I think, was the sentiment they conveyed just then, determined hatred, and a shade of disappointment and chagrin. She had fancied Louie had been kept in the Study all the morning or had been sent to the Bishop, and here she found her sleeping quietly in the dormitory, with her head on her hand, and a happy smile on her lips.

"I'll pay you yet, miss, for what you said this morning," she whispered, as she leaned on the foot of the bed and gazed at her. "Some way 'ill turn up; I'll make you sorry for it yet."

A way turned up very soon; the devil isn't slow in giving work to those who are waiting for it.

After Addy had gazed her fill at her unconscious enemy, she turned away and applied herself to what had brought her up to the dormitory at this unusual time of day. She opened her trunk cautiously, took out a book, and shutting it again, went over and seated herself by the window, and, secreting the book in her apron very dexterously, and leaning her head on her hand, she was soon lost in the perusal of it. The fact was, novels were *contre les règles* at St. Mary's Hall—that is, indiscriminate and second-rate novels were. The Waverleys and some other standard works of fiction were in the Hall library, to which the girls had always access. But the reading of the promiscuous yellow-covered literature with which the country is flooded, was most strictly and most righteously forbidden, and in the decree all the right-minded girls in the school acquiesced. There were some, however, who still clung fondly to the "Lost Heiress," the "Deserted Bride," a "Heart Unmasked," and others of the same stamp.

Adelaide was among their warmest advocates, and had come back this term well supplied with this contraband literature, which she had quietly circulated among intimate and appreciative friends. Several volumes had been discovered in their hands and confiscated, but, of course, they were too "honorable" to betray the real owner, and Adelaide had entirely escaped suspicion. Indeed, she had a peculiar talent for *escaping*—perhaps we may call it her only talent, her only shining one, at least; but it did her good service—helped her to maintain a fair standing in the school—to keep "in" with her teachers, and with the girls, on amicable terms, if not in actual friendship.

"It's my opinion," cried one of her wretched accomplices in a down town expedition, who had been detected and brought to justice, "that if the whole world should burn up, Addy McFarlane would stand without a hair singed!"

That was a little extravagant, perhaps, but really it did seem to describe the case pretty well. She seemed to bear a charmed life—to be invulnerable to justice—unattainable by malice; she slipped through the teachers' fingers, worked her way silently out of scrapes, did an immense deal of mischief in the school, and was very comfortable and complacent as she went along.

The bell rang. "There, I must go," she thought, regretfully, as she rose slowly, and, reading as she went, walked toward her trunk. Half-way across the room she stopped, too much absorbed to give up the book. The heroine was eloping; she was stealing down past her cruel parents' door to her faithful Everard's arms; a travelling carriage stood behind a clump of trees, not five minutes' walk from the house; the night was black and starless; oh! *would* she get down safe!

When — Adelaide gave a violent start — the handle of the door turned, not the door of the heroine's parents' room, but, which concerned her much more nearly, her own proper, particular dormitory-door; and quick as a flash she threw the book on the bed nearest which she stood; it was Louie's; she gave it a push that sent it within three inches of her hand, sprung across to her own bed, and before Miss Barlow was fairly in the room, was kneeling tranquilly before her trunk, with half its contents spread on the floor beside her, busily engaged in arranging and assorting a pile of under-clothes.

"Why, Adelaide! Is that you? I did not see you. What are you doing up here at this hour? The bell has rung."

"I know it, ma'am, and I am hurrying as fast as I can. I came up for a clean handkerchief, and I found my trunk in such disorder that I couldn't help stopping to fix it a little. I put it in order last Saturday; I don't see how I've managed to tumble it so."

The teacher gave her neatness an approving smile; none of the others thought of arranging theirs oftener than once a week, and only then by compulsion. It was really quite delightful to see a girl who cared at all about the order her things were in, and Miss Barlow said as much. Addy took the praise demurely, and looked much grati-

2*

fied, hurrying through the undertaking, neverthe-less, with all convenient speed. Before she had accomplished it, however, and reached the door, Miss Barlow had accomplished what she considered the detection of the unlucky Louie's guilt.

Miss Barlow's expression on seeing the quiet, easy sleep of the culprit, was not as entirely unlike Adelaide's, when she first witnessed the same phenomenon, as Miss Barlow's admirers could have wished. It did not seem to gratify her at all; in-deed, I may say, she looked as if she was very much exasperated, and as if she thought it sheer impertinence in Louie to forget her troubles in sleep, and a shameful perversion of the ends of justice.

It is also unpleasant to acknowledge, but there was something very like a gleam of triumph in her eyes as they lit on the book which had ap-parently but just slipped from the sleeper's hand. You know it is so pleasant to find we have not been mistaken. Such an occurrence as this seems a direct compliment to our sagacity—a confirmation of our best opinion of our own penetration. We must not blame Miss Barlow too much for her complacency in this matter.

"I thought as much," she murmured, as she read the title. "I have seen for some time past the working of this poisonous stuff in her mind. This explains all. Adelaide," she continued, aloud, "do you know how Louie came by this book?" holding it up.

Adelaide shook her head. "I have seen it lying around for some time, ma'am, but I couldn't say precisely where it came from. Louie brought some books back with her, I know."

"Others of this description, do you mean?"

Adelaide looked down. "I am not much with Louie, ma'am. I do not know a great deal about her reading or anything she does. I can't say precisely anything about her books."

"I see how it is; you are unwilling to expose her. I respect the feeling you have, and shall not press the matter now, but if I am obliged to call you up about it, I shall expect you to tell me the whole truth. However unpleasant it may be, you must remember it will be your duty."

Adelaide bowed and hurried out. This idea was exactly the one she had meant to convey to Miss Barlow, and she entered the schoolroom with quite a radiant expression; it was wonderful how well things had worked.

Meantime, Miss Barlow had placed the book under lock and key, and after lingering a moment by the sleeping girl as if she longed to bring her back to reality again, she turned and left the room; and Louie slept quietly on.

CHAPTER III.

CLOUDY.

"Oh! 'tis easy
"To beget great deeds; but in the rearing of them—
The threading in cool blood each mean detail,
And furze-brake of half pertinent circumstance—
There lies the self-denial."

KINGSLEY.

THE Study again, if you please, but this time
with more august occupants. Teachers' meeting
was just over; the Bishop, patient and attentive,
had for the last two hours listened to the reports,
suggestions and complaints of some twenty-five
teachers, male and female; had entered calmly, and
thoughtfully into the merits of each case, advised,
arranged, revised, with clearness and precision; had
bent his mind as entirely to the settling of the
slightest of the many slight difficulties that arose,
as if his mind had had no other cares or plans upon
it; as if this school, and the government of it,
were the sole duties of his life, instead of being, as
was the truth, about the fiftieth part of that which
came upon him daily.

There was a little weariness in the gesture, perhaps, as leaning back in his chair as the last one left the room, he passed his hand across his forehead and closed his eyes for a moment. Only a moment, however, for looking up, he said to Mr. Rogers, who had remained:

"I want to speak to you a moment before I go, about one of the children whose expression I have noticed lately. I do not like it, it is very unhappy and haggard for one of her age. Do you know anything about her—Louisa Atterbury?"

"It was of her I wished to speak to you. She has not been brought particularly under my notice till lately. Last term, which was her first, she was an average good girl, did very well in her studies, and always had a tolerable, though never very high mark for conduct. But this summer, the complaints of her bad temper and unruliness, have been uncomfortably frequent, and she has fallen off too, in attention to her studies. The teacher who has charge of the dormitory she is in, indeed, has been to me several times with complaints, about the justice of which, I think, there can be no doubt."

"And none about their judiciousness? She is in Miss Barlow's dormitory, if I remember right, and I have sometimes feared that Miss Barlow had not quite the self-control and discretion that her office

needs. However, perhaps there has been no want
of them in this case. I cannot judge. You say the
girl has been self-willed and rebellious?"

Mr. Rogers briefly related the occurrence of the
morning, and added, that he rather feared for the
result of the reprieve; he thought that she could
not be brought to apologize and explain to Miss
Barlow; he thought he saw that much in her eyes
when she left the room. And in case of her continued refusal, of course, there was nothing for him
to do but to send her officially to him, the Bishop,
for judgment and reproof.

"I would desire you to avoid that, if possible,"
said the Bishop, thoughtfully. "It will be very
much of a disgrace, and may do her more injury
than too much laxity would. She does not look, to
me, like a viciously stubborn child; I should trust
very much to her good feelings, if they can be
worked upon; gentleness and consideration may do
much for her."

"They have been tried, sir."

"I do not doubt it, but try them once again. I
should advise you seeing her alone to-morrow morning, without the aggravation of her teacher's
presence. Let her feel that it is a desire for her
good and not a stubborn love of authority, that
actuates those to whom she is bound to submit; and

once convinced of that, I am very much mistaken in my reading of her face, if she does not yield."

"I trust you are right sir, but if she does not?"

"If she does not, of course you must send her to me; but avoid it, if possible."

It was in accordance with this advice that Mr. Rogers, entering the Study next morning after Chapel, said to Miss Barlow, who, with her pupil, was awaiting him:

"I would like to have a few minutes' conversation with Louisa alone, Miss Barlow. May I ask you to leave her with me?"

This was as unwelcome as it was unexpected to the teacher, but there was nothing to be said, and nothing to be done, but to obey.

"Sit down a moment, Louisa," said Mr. Rogers, in a kind tone; "I have a note to answer, it will not detain me long."

Mr. Rogers sat down to his writing, Louie to her thoughts. And they were gentler thoughts than hers had been lately. There was nothing of sternness or anger in the thoughtful face of her judge, no haste or irritation in his movements; perhaps he meant her kindly: and as she had just come from Chapel, perhaps the better resolutions of yesterday had been renewed there as she knelt; and there was no one at hand to rouse the newly conquered

obstinacy. At all events, when Mr. Rogers raised
his eyes from his note, he saw Louie's were full of
tears, though she turned her head quickly away,
and he rose and approached her kindly.

"I hope," he said, "that the time you have had
to think about our conversation yesterday, has resulted in a determination to do as you know I
desire you to do. I am not apt to be unreasonable,
am I? And I think you must have seen, if you
have thought about it, that this is not unreasonable.
How is it?"

Louie hung her head. "No, sir, perhaps it isn't
unreasonable."

"But you think it is hard, Louie! Duty gene-
erally is, my child, and self-abasement is the hard-
est duty I know ; but you do not require to be told
what its reward is, what blessed promise is to him
'who humbleth himself.' And rebellion and
pride, Louie, never profited any one yet. Fretting
and struggling only make the yoke more galling
(for a yoke of some kind there must be), whereas,
submission and patience make it endurable and
easy."

Louie knew all that, and a great deal else that
Mr. Rogers said to her before, but it came with
new force from his lips now, and she answered in a
changed and humbled voice:

"I will try, sir, to do as you require. I will ask Miss Barlow's pardon—but—is it asking too much —may I write to her instead of speaking to her about it? If you would allow me "——

Mr. Rogers looked thoughtfully at her.

"Why, Louie?"

She colored as she answered, and bit her lip.

"I am afraid to trust myself, sir. I know it's very wrong, but when I'm with Miss Barlow, I can't do as I meant to before; I always get angry and impertinent."

"I am willing," said Mr. Rogers, after a moment's pause. "You may write your apology, if you choose."

He handed her a sheet of paper and a pen. Just then the bell rang for breakfast.

"Will you come down to the table or write your note first?"

"I'd rather write the note first, if you please."

"Very well; some breakfast shall be saved for you. When your note is finished, leave it on the table. I will see that Miss Barlow receives it."

The note, short as it was, cost Louie much time and thought, and it was only just completed when the girls came up from breakfast. This is a "true copy" of it:

"MISS BARLOW:

"Mr. Rogers has given me permission to write to you and make the explanation you asked me for yesterday. The reason I was late in Chapel was that I had a book down in my desk that I wanted to read in. I was dressed some time before the others, and ran down to the school-room before the bell began to ring. I didn't notice when it stopped; they had all gone into Chapel before I thought anything about it.

"I have also to apologize for my conduct in refusing an explanation. I now see it was improper, and am sorry for it. .

"L. R. ATTERBURY."

This note, folded and directed, but unsealed, she left on the Study table, and went out with a very much lighter heart than she had known what it was to have for some days. The Matron, with whom she was something of a favorite, had ordered her breakfast saved, and she ate it alone in the huge dining-room with considerable appetite and much comfort.

Oh, the difference between an easy conscience and a burdened one! Louie went upstairs two steps at a time; she ran through the hall humming "Brightest Eyes;" at the schoolroom door she brushed against Alice Aulay, who, with her arms full of books, was hurrying out; and, as a natural consequence of the collision, half the books went flying over the floor.

"Oh, Ally! don't scold," cried Louie, stooping to pick them up.

"I think you might look a little where you go, though," said Alice, regarding, very much troubled, the *débris* on the floor.

"I think I might, too," returned Louie, good-humoredly, "only I never do, somehow. Why, child, you've got more than you can carry; your little arms will break. Where are you taking them to?"

"I'm taking 'em to Julia Alison and Laura Boutwell. They are in Miss Stanton's room."

"Here; I'll help you. I'll take these."

When they reached the door of Miss Stanton's room, Louie paused for a moment. Laura Boutwell and Julia were writing busily at the table. Julia looked up for an instant, but seeing Louie, dropped her eyes and went on with her work. Louie walked up to the table and said, laying the books down:

"These come consigned to you, I think, Laura. There was a collision at the schoolroom door, attended with great damage to the cargo of the

'Alice,' but I acted with much gallantry and presence of mind on the occasion, and was able to rescue something from the wreck."

"Many thanks," said Laura, looking up with a smile. "I suppose we ought to make you a neat speech and vote you a service of plate; that's what humane people generally get; don't they?"

"According to the newspapers," answered Louie, lingering a moment and looking at Julia, who never raised her eyes nor smiled, but wrote on persistently. With a little sigh, she turned and left the room. "That was unkind," she thought, as she walked slowly back to the schoolroom. It was the first damp her new spirits had received.

Addy McFarlane, at the time of "the collision," had been engaged in a little privateering enterprise in the schoolroom. Her desk was next to Louie's, and as she happened to know that Louie had her *thème* written out, she naturally thought it would save her a good deal of trouble, if she could find it, to copy it off entire, for Louie's were generally the best exercises in the class. She was just engaged in rummaging through the wilderness of her desk in pursuit of it, when Alice's exclamation and Louie's voice made her start up and drop the desk-lid. She seized the nearest book and devoted herself to it till the two withdrew from the scene;

then she returned to the charge. But on lifting the lid of the desk, it was with some chagrin that she discovered the unfortunate results of her precipitate retreat. A bottle of ink had been upset, and had damaged considerably an adjacent pile of copy-books, but the chief sufferer was a prettily bound little volume which had lain beside it.

"Unlucky!" thought Adelaide; "very unlucky!"

She mopped up the current ink with her handkerchief and a piece of paper, shoved the injured copy-books into the background, put the stopper in the ink-bottle, pulled a slate over the daubed bottom of the desk, and ejaculated complacently: "There, nobody'd guess anything had happened. It's as good as ever—only this tiresome book—what *shall* I do with it?"

She gave a furtive glance around; the room was nearly empty. The two girls at the other end, toward the door, were sitting with their backs to her. Concealing her handkerchief and book under her apron, she hurried up to a closet at the upper end of the room that was seldom or never used—the bottom part of it, at least. She flung them in and shut the door, reflecting as she regained her seat: "Nobody'll ever be the wiser."

The bell rung, and the schoolroom filled rapidly. Louie, hurrying in, took her seat, and whispering,

" Oh, Adelaide ! have you found the 'Word for the
Day ?' " pushed up the lid of her desk and began a
rapid search for the Bible.

" Yes—yes," returned Adelaide, very officiously,
" here it is ; look over and learn it with me."

For the ink wasn't dry yet, she thought with
alarm.

Louie took hold of the proffered Bible, and the
two heads bent over it very earnestly for several
minutes, and when Mr. Rogers entered and the
whole school rose to say the " Word for the Day,"
Addy repeated it as glibly and correctly as any one
else did.   Louie stumbled a little in reciting it, but
it rung in her ears all day.

" Before destruction the heart of man is haughty ;
and before honor is humility."

Louie almost thought Mr. Rogers' eyes were on
her all the while that he explained it; that may
have been fancy, but his thoughts certainly were.

Though painfully exemplifying Louie's want of
neatness in the arrangement of her desk, truth com-
pels me to state that she did not perceive the recent
invasion of it.   Her visits to it were hurried (Louie
generally was in a hurry), and it presented such a
distracting maze of confusion, that she was glad to
drop the lid and forget it the instant she had found
the book she wanted.

The only time that she came near discovering the mishap, was in the French class, the last recitation before school closed. She chanced to be seated between Addy and Julia; it was a chance she would have avoided if she could, for they were, for very different reasons, the two girls whose neighborhood was least pleasant to her. Addy she always shunned for very obvious reasons, and Julia, whenever they had met during the day, had shown so unmistakable a coldness that all Louie's pride was roused, and nothing could have been more vexatious than the discovery that she made after her hurried entrance and appropriation of the nearest vacant seat, that it was bounded on the east by Adelaide McFarlane's grey *foulard*, and on the west by Julia Alison's pale blue muslin. She bit her lip in vexation, said "bother!" under her breath, glanced around to see if it were possible to change, but finding it was not, arranged her books and submitted to her fate.

Miss Marbais, a brisk little Frenchwoman, who never allowed the loss of a minute in her class, began the lesson promptly. She plunged them into " *dictée*," without a thought of mercy and with a cruel rapidity, and all wits had a hard race to follow in her wake. Louie did not mind it very much; "she took to French," the girls said, "as ducks take to water;" it never was the least trouble for her to

prepare the lessons that gave some of her companions such extreme perplexity, and as for dictation, it was as easy to her as so much English
would have been. Julia, also, was a good scholar,
probably a more thorough one than Louie; but
Addy McFarlane found the half hour devoted to
dictée the time that tried her soul most unbearably.
Miss Marbais was very wide awake, nothing ever
seemed to escape her, and Adelaide being a very
indifferent French scholar, had much ado to shuffle
along respectably among her more advanced companions. We have seen how she managed the
thème business; translation was something of a
bugbear, but by dint of studying over the passage
that was coming to her, and managing dexterously
about getting a seat near some person not prin-
cipled against prompting, she escaped open disgrace in that part of the hour's exercises, but at
dictation she was hopelessly routed. More than
once, her horribly incorrect rendering of Miss
Marbais' rapid French had been held up to public
derision. The silence that reigned during the lesson was too entire to admit of prompting, and
indeed every girl was too busy on her own account
to give any help to a bewildered neighbor.

On this particular occasion she had twisted herself into rather an ungraceful attitude, but one

which enabled her to glance over Louie's slate, and she was availing herself greedily of the opportunity, till Louie, perceiving the advantage her adversary was taking of her labors, rather pettishly turned away and put her slate beyond the reach of Adelaide's anxious eyes. But Adelaide followed, and in a few minutes was again copying rapidly from her slate. Louie perceived it, and mentally exclaiming:

"She's the meanest girl I ever knew! If she will do such things, she shall pay for them."

And with a rapid pencil she wrote on, in the most absurd French she could think of, and ingeniously introduced as many laughable mistakes as the subject admitted of. She knew she could correct her own slate before Miss Marbais asked for it, and her familiarity with the language made it quite easy for her to play off this very questionable trick upon her ancient foe. The subject which Miss Marbais had chosen, was Mary Queen of Scots' adieu to France, and the vehement little Frenchwoman, no doubt, looked upon the horrible mangling and mutilation of these pretty verses as a sacrilegious thing, for as her eye glanced over Adelaide's slate, her face underwent many rapid changes from grave to gay, from lively to severe, and many broken

3

exclamations in alternate French and English, burst from her lips. At last, while Adelaide with suspended breath watched her apprehensively and Louie smothered her laughter, she tapped on the desk, and holding up the slate, exclaimed:

" *O malheureuse princesse!* *Ecoutez, mesdemoiselles.*"

And with much gesticulation and cruel emphasis, she read off the absurd jumble of nonsense to the eagerly attentive girls. The result of course, was an unequivocal burst of laughter, and curious whispers of " Whose is it—whose is it?"

" *C'est à Mademoiselle McFarlane,*" responded Miss Marbais without note or comment, as she laid it down.

"Justly celebrated for her early proficiency in the language," laughed Louie very low.

It would, indeed, have made poor Marie Stuart's hair stand on end, I am afraid; her "listening spirit" wouldn't altogether have "rejoiced" in this rendering of her adieu; the girls said as much as this, in stage asides, and a good deal more to the same effect, and it was some time before they could be quieted to study again. In the meanwhile, Addy's face, which had not turned red, but rather white, had shown no discomposure, but had been bent eagerly toward the teacher, awaiting the moment when she should read Louie's. verses, thinking, "I'll have good company in my disgrace when she gets to *them*."

But when Miss Marbais did get to them, and reading them quietly over, returned them to Louie with a "*Très bien fait*," the whole truth flashed upon her. The glare of malice that filled her eyes no one saw; they lit on Louie for an instant, who was now intent on her *thème*, then they dropped upon her book.

"You shall pay dearly for this, *chérie*," she murmured inaudibly.

In a few moments, Miss Marbais, who had begun correcting the exercises, put out her hand for Louie's, going on with her work of looking over another's, and not raising her eyes. Meanwhile the luckless Louie had opened her exercise-book, and had discovered its fair pages miserably defaced with huge daubs of ink, indeed, so much defaced that the *thème* for that day was almost unintelligible.

"How could I have done it!" she ejaculated in consternation. A faint hope of repairing the damage by dint of scratching out some blots and re-writing some lines inspired her to long for a few minutes' delay, and she glanced anxiously toward her neighbors to see whose exercise might be substituted for hers, pro tem. Adelaide held hers,

neatly written in her hand, ready to give to Miss
Marbais when demanded. Of her, of course, she
could not now ask a favor; she turned to Julia,
who sat with her pretty white hands folded before
her, her *livre de thème* lying on her knee. If Louie
had not been so miserably cornered, she never
would have been driven into doing what she did at
that moment. Nothing but the dread of laying
that horrible *thème* before Miss Marbais would have
betrayed her into asking a favor of Julia. Forget-
ting everything but Miss Marbais, she leant down
and whispered eagerly :

"Give her yours. I want to fix mine before she
sees it."

Miss Marbais' hand was still extended: she
moved it a little impatiently, still with her eyes on
the book before her, and said :

"*Mademoiselle, votre thème, vite.*"

Louie gave a despairing glance toward Julia.
Her quietly folded hands never stirred a hair's
breadth; a slight glow of color on her half-averted
face alone showed that she had heard Louie speak.
The very angriest feelings that had ever filled Louie's
heart rushed into it then, as she sprung up and
handed Miss Marbais her exercise, open at the
worst page.

"Now, Julia and I are done with each other forever; if I live a hundred years, I can never forget that—never!"

If she could have seen into Julia's heart at that moment, she would have repented of her hasty judgment; of the two, perhaps, she suffered most in this new estrangement, and only saw her error when too late, her pride told her, to remedy it. When Louie hurriedly asked her for her exercise, she imagined that it was to give her time to make some corrections she had discovered necessary since coming to class, from looking over some book that Miss Marbais had corrected. Surprise and shame at Louie's want of honor, and a conscientiousness about being a party to any such deceptions, had kept her silent during the brief instant that Louie had turned to her for help. Only when Miss Marbais took up the book and, turning to its proprietor, demanded the cause of the state she found it in, did she see her error.

"I don't know how it happened, ma'am," said Louie, speaking hurriedly; "I didn't see it till I came to class."

"That's odd," said Miss Marbais, rather sharply. "It's really surprising how many things happen to you that you cannot possibly account for. It strikes me *I* should know it if I had spilt a bottle of ink over one of my books; perhaps it will help you to remember it another time, to rewrite this before you have any dinner. You may try it, at all events."

Louie's cheeks burned as she took back the book. Miss Marbais had always been perfectly just and kind to her before, and this certainly was just. She did not say a word, but she bit her lip as she thought: "Whether I try or not, it's all one. Everything goes wrong."

They had about ten minutes in the schoolroom before school was dismissed; Louie had seized her grammar and *cahier* and was trying to make up for the error, and make the most of the ten minutes, but never had her work been so hard; she was excited and nervous, and could not put her mind on what she was about, and Adelaide McFarlane's eyes danced as she watched her angrily tear the third page out of her copy-book, blotted and incorrect. Adelaide could not forbear a little curiosity about the matter, and watched narrowly, and wondered much that Louie did not avail herself of three corrected exercises that lay within reach of her hand, their owners absent, too. What a stupid girl, to miss such a chance!

About three minutes before the bell rung for the dismissal of school, a servant entered the room, and, with a card in her hand, walked down to the desk of the teacher in charge, and said, "there was a lady and gentleman in the parlor to see Miss Atter bury."

Louie's quick ears caught her name; she waited, trembling with excitement (for visitors to Miss Atterbury were angelic in their infrequency—few and far between) till the teacher called her up, and delivering the card to her, said graciously :

"You may go to the parlor without waiting for the dismissing of school."

Louie read the name and gave an ecstatic " Hurrah!" under her breath, and danced down the schoolroom, forgetful of proprieties.

The teacher smiled a little ; she had been young herself—perhaps at no very distant date. She said to Adelaide:

" You may put away Louie's books that she has left about. She will not want them again this afternoon."

"She hasn't finished her exercise," answered Adelaide, quickly. " Miss Marbais sent her up to write it over before she can come to dinner."

" Ah!" said the teacher, looking serious. " However, you may put them away for the present."

And Adelaide shuffled them into the desk with no very tender hand.

CHAPTER IV.

THE SUN COMES OUT.

"Who knows whither the clouds have fled?
  In the unscarred heaven they leave no wake;
And the eyes forget the tears they have shed,
  The heart forgets its sorrow and ache."

LOWELL.

AT the parlor-door, Louie paused a moment in a great flutter of excitement; but a small boy, who had been keeping watch for her approach, darted out and dragged her in.

"Oh, you wretched Tom!" she cried, as she flew into the arms of a lady standing just within the door. "Why didn't you give me time to compose my nerves before I came in?"

"Your hair needs it more, dear," said the urchin.

"Oh, my hair!" she exclaimed, holding up the heavy braids with one hand while she gave the other to the tall gentleman who stood looking down at her with a smile.

"Not cured of your carelessness yet, eh, Louie?" he said.

"No, sir; I begin to think it has become chronic," she answered, with a laugh that eventuated in a low, uneasy sigh. "But I am so surprised to see you!"

"And so glad?"

"Ah, sir!"

"Why, of course, Uncle Rawdon, she's glad," Tom interposed.

"That is, I would have been, sir, if you'd left Tom at home."

"Louie, my dear girl," said Tom, thrusting his hands into his pockets, and putting great expression in his little, old, odd face, "we had hoped to find that boarding-school had taken some of the sauciness out of you, whereas it is but too clear, at even the first glance, that you are as bad as ever."

"Ingrate! never ask me to hem another set of sails for you."

"I shan't, you may be sure, for those you did in the spring ripped out the first time I tried 'em."

"Oh! oh!"

"Tom, will you be quiet and let us talk to Louie?" exclaimed his mother, drawing the girl affectionately toward her as they sat down on the sofa. "Never mind the hair, Louie, we've seen it so before, you know. But you're not looking well, child. I am sure, now your face is quiet that you

3*

look paler than when you left us.   Don't you think
so, Rawdon?"

"A little, perhaps," said the gentleman, looking
at her thoughtfully.   "Have you been studying
too hard, Louie?"

"Anything but that," she returned, hastily, col-
oring a little.   "I am very well, though, I assure
you, only so surprised at seeing you I can hardly
speak.   It is so nice—how did you happen to think
about coming here?   I thought you were on your
way to Canada before this time."

"We are *en route* for the Lakes now," explained
the lady, "and as we shall be away all summer, we
could not go without running down here for a
night to see you and say good bye.   Tom gave
me no peace either; saucy as he is, now he's with
you."

"Mamma, don't flatter Louie.   I wanted to see
you, my dear, to tell you that your letters are getting very blue and tiresome, and if you can't write
anything more spicy and jolly, I think you had
better discontinue altogether.   Uncle Rawdon
thinks so too, I know."

"Louie knows better than that," said Col. Ruthven.   "Louie knows that her letters are always
welcome, even if they are homesick and 'blue' as
Tom says they are getting to be.   I hope he is mis-

taken, though, about it; surely you are not homesick ?"

Col. Ruthven saw in a moment that he had
touched an aching chord; so, before Louie could get
out her hesitating answer, he tried to divert the
conversation into another channel, and succeeded
so well that in a few moments Louie herself had
forgotten that there was such a word as homesick
in general use, or such a sentiment in circulation;
and, in recalling the delights of last spring, the
adventures, the jokes, the entertainments of that
happy time, the present dullness and recent wretchedness of school life, were quite obliterated. She
only remembered them, when Col. Ruthven, in his
quick way, said she must go and ask for a holiday;
they would not insist upon her having longer leave
than till the next day at noon; but Mr. Rogers
would not refuse that, he was sure.

"Yes, go quick, there's not a minute to lose,"
urged Tom. "We're going to do lots of things, and
Uncle Rawdon has ordered dinner at the hotel at
half-past three, and we shall have to make good
time to get back for it. Oh what makes you so
slow ? One would think you were afraid of Mr.
Rogers."

"No, I'm not afraid," said Louie falteringly, as
she moved toward the door. "I'm not afraid, only

I don't know whether I can go—Mr. Rogers may
think—I don't know "——

"But you can ask him," said Col. Ruthven, with
a kind smile as he opened the door for her. "Tell
him who has come for you, and promise to study
extra well for the next week, and I think he won't
refuse you—I couldn't, I know," he added in a low
tone as he closed the door and turned to the window.

The young ne'er-do-weel, in the moment that
intervened between the closing of the parlor door
and the opening of the study door, did not feel the
same confidence; she trembled and faltered as she
stood before Mr. Rogers, who was busy at his writing, and who had hardly noticed her first faint
knock.   He looked up.

"Ah, Louie; what is it?"

She could hardly get the words out; it was so
absurd for her to be coming to this room, to ask
a favor of Mr. Rogers, a special indulgence, when
she had so lately left it in disgrace.   .

" I came to ask you, sir, if I might go and dine
and stay till to-morrow with some friends who
have just arrived. I am sorry, sir—I know I
ought not to ask—but I don't go out very often—
I haven't many chances—and if you could be so
good—this time"——

Mr. Rogers laid down his pen and looked at her attentively.

"Who has come for you?"

"My godmother, Mrs. Appleton, with whom I spent my vacation in the spring, and her brother, Col. Ruthven. They're the only people who ever come to see me, you know, sir, and they're going away to Canada to be gone all summer—I shan't see them again in ever so long. They only want me to stay till noon to-morrow."

"Well, Louie, I don't mean to seem harsh, but think a moment. Does a holiday seem to come well on the top of such a week as this has been? Could you blame me if I said I could not reward such conduct as yours has been lately?"

"No—oh no, sir," said Louie, with a quivering lip. "I didn't think you'd let me go—I know it's all right," and she turned away.

"Stay a moment, Louie. If I thought this indulgence would do you no harm—if you would only see in it my desire to do you good and make you happy, perhaps I might allow it this time. Would you really try to make yourself worthy of the confidence, if I made the experiment?"

"I think you would never see any cause to be sorry, sir; I meant to do better before, and this will only make me try the harder to please you."

"Very well, then, you have my consent."

"Oh, thank you, sir!" and Louie with a very glowing face was turning away, when a sudden extinction of the smiles, and a gradual paling of the excited flush on her cheek, indicated that she had thought of something that might change Mr. Rogers' decree. That something was the miserable *thème* now lying uncommenced on her desk. With a sigh she thought, "That settles it!" and then turning again to the clergyman, she said:

"I had forgotten, sir; I ought to tell you, I have not done my French exercise. Miss Marbais said I must do it before dinner for a punishment."

"Then that alters it entirely. I cannot interfere again between you and your teacher. You must see I cannot excuse you again. If you have been inattentive to-day you must take the consequences of it. I am sorry for you—I wish it were otherwise, but I cannot reconcile it to my conscience to indulge you to-day."

Mr. Rogers spoke quickly; he did not want to have his resolution shaken by another look at the girl's imploring eyes; so he put considerable decision into his tones, and without looking at her again, resumed his writing, and said she might go.

She did go, hurriedly enough, shutting the door

very quickly, and only stopping when half-way across to the parlor. What should she say to them—what would they think of her? Oh! it was too cruel—disgracing her before the people that she cared more for than all the rest of the world put together except mother—denying her the only holiday she would have all summer long. How could she go into the parlor, her face all red with crying, and tell them how it was, and why she was refused what any other girl would have been allowed?

The summer wind swept through the wide hall; oh! how sweet it looked outside! Not a soul was near; it was as quiet as if there were not a busy multitude within a hundred yards of where she stood. But all were collected in the schoolroom now; she felt safe as she heard the distant buzz of voices there, and turning back irresolutely, she approached the staircase, and, sitting down on the lowest step, buried her face in her hands.

She had meant to quiet herself and gain composure by this respite, but "thinking it over" only made it worse; before she could think, she was sobbing hopelessly.

"Oh! what shall I do!" as the sobs came thicker and faster. "I shall never get over it enough to go in; I never can stop when once I get crying.

I wouldn't have them see me for the world. Oh, it is too miserable!"

But through it all, Louie's honest heart told her it was all right—there was no injustice here; no injustice, only, as she thought, her unhappy, pursuing fate. She wished she could die and be rid of all the wretchedness of her life; she was sick of being always wrong and always ashamed of her wrongdoings. Was there no remedy for this—would there be no end to it?

A hand was laid gently on her head; she started up and took her hands from before her face for a moment, then pressed them back with double shame; it was the Bishop.

"Child, what is it? You are not afraid to tell me?"

No, Louie was not afraid; the strong, clear voice that she had hardly ever heard before out of church or chapel, addressing all the others, warning, advising, directing all at once, now speaking to her alone, was so low, so gentle, she hardly knew it for the same. It cast out all fear from her heart; she could have told him all, and tried, only the words would not come and the sobs would. She raised her head and made a strong effort to speak; said something unintelligible about Mr. Rogers, then broke down altogether, and hid her face in her hands.

"You have just come from the Study? Then come back there with me, and Mr. Rogers shall tell me about it."

He took her hand and led her to the Study door; Mr. Rogers' "Come in" was not so awful this time; indeed, there was nothing awful in the world now, since what had been to her the embodiment of awe and terror, held her by the hand as if she were indeed his child, and soothed her in a voice that had an echo of the tenderness to which she had so long been unused.

It was all extremely dreamy, and Louie could never distinctly recall it afterward; Mr. Rogers' explanation—the Bishop's intercession for her—the sudden reversal of her sentence—were things too deliriously delightful to be distinct. In five minutes she was flying up the stairs, not looking like the cousin sixteen times removed to the girl who had just been sitting at the foot of them, sobbing in such a broken-hearted fashion. She burst into the dormitory, now filled with girls washing off the day's ink and dust before dinner, and springing over trunks and beds, pulled open her wardrobe and flung out upon the bed her pink muslin, white mantilla and straw hat.

"Heigho!" cried Addy, the soap slipping from her hands, as in concert with the rest of the room, she stared in amazement at the rapid movements of the new-comer. "What are you going to do with your best clothes at this time of day?"

"Put them on, if you've no objection," returned Louie, unlacing her boots with such vigor that the tag went click-click through the holes with the precision and rapidity of an eight-day clock ticking with all its might.

"How about Miss Marbais? Does she know you're going out without writing the exercise she gave you to do before dinner?" demanded Adelaide, in a voice purposely raised so as to be audible to Miss Barlow, who sat at her window at the other end of the room.

"I haven't told her; I knew you'd enjoy running down and mentioning it so much; do go!"

"Thank you, I've better business; only I bet Mr. Rogers didn't know of it when he gave you leave."

Louie was too secure and too happy to care for this; indeed she rather enjoyed Adelaide's spite and vexation; so she only shrugged her shoulders and looked very mischievous, and begged her of all things not to tell! And she sprung up and made a hurried assault upon the basin and pitcher; but the pitcher was very full, and the reckless way in which she poured the water into the basin, of course resulted in dispensing three-quarters of it around the adjacent washstands. Alice Aulay's was the greatest sufferer, and the little girl herself received a good dash of it on her clean white apron, and Julia, who was curling her hair for her, made an involuntary exclamation of dismay, perhaps reproach.

Alice had been pretty near a cry for the last half hour, owing to a want of success in her geography lesson, and an accumulation of distresses resulting from her failure in those "map questions" which had for the last week made her life a burden to her; and now this little *contretemps* was all that was needed to send her into an ecstasy of weeping. She hid her face in Julia's dress and screamed as only very small and very unreasonable children can scream; and amid passionate laments for her wet apron, she mingled incoherent reproaches of Louie Atterbury as "the hatefullest girl in school"—the cause of all her troubles, and "too mean for anything."

Julia tried to soothe her, and ventured to say, she had not meant to do it.

"She did mean to do it!" cried the child. "She's always doing things, and she always means to do 'em! She knocked down my books this morning. She's hateful—she's always teasing me!"

"I know she's careless, Ally; but you mustn't be cross."

Louie turned sharply round at this, and said, angrily:

"You have had the greatest hand in spoiling that child. I blame you more than her that she is the torment of the dormitory. Alice, if you don't stop, I'll report you; be quiet now—its enough to drive one wild to hear that howling—be quiet; do you hear?"

Of course, as might have been expected, this had the effect of redoubling Alice's screams; and Julia, quite roused at Louie's injustice and unkindness, kept her arms around her little *protégée*, and spoke in a low, fondling tone to her, that was quite exasperating to the originator of the uproar. Addy McFarlane, sitting on the foot of her bed, laughed in a very provoking way, and begged everybody's pardon, but, it struck her, good-temper had of late been at a premium in the dormitory; and Miss Barlow, hurrying down the room, asked, in a sharp, high key, what all the noise was about.

None seemed to consider themselves exactly qualified to answer this question. Alice subdued her sobs a little, Julia turned away as if it were not her business to explain, the others all stood spectator fashion, looking at Louie.

"I suppose it's all about me, ma'am," that young person answered, in default of anybody else, going on, however, with the business of washing her hands. "I was unlucky enough to spatter some water on small Miss Aulay's pinafore, and she has been entertaining us since the occurrence with some very energetic squalling. I didn't enjoy it as much as Julia seemed to, and so threatened to report her, if she didn't stop, which only produced renewed excitement. I am sorry if it disturbed you, ma'am."

"It *did* disturb me, and I shall take pains to prevent its recurrence. Alice, whenever Louie annoys you, come to me immediately, and I will see that you have justice done you. Such disturbances in my dormitory are a disgrace to me. You may come to me after dinner, Louisa, about this little matter; we will settle it at leisure."

"I shall not be here after dinner, ma'am. I am going out to dinner."

"Who gave you permission to go?

"Mr. Rogers, ma'am."

"Did he know of your French exercise?"

"Not till I told him of it."

"Do you mean to say, Mr. Rogers made it no objection to your having a holiday that you were under punishment for the second time to-day?"

"He did make it an objection, ma'am, and said at first I could not go."

"And what induced him to change his mind, pray?"

· "Why, ma'am, the Bishop asked him to excuse me."

It is impossible to convey the tone of subdued triumph in which this "settler" was brought out; the effect upon the audience was strong and instantaneous, and Miss Barlow changed color angrily, but attempted no reply. The bell fortunately rang for dinner at that moment, and a sudden change of feeling occurred. Unfinished toilettes were hurriedly dispatched, and "all hands" started for the door within as few seconds as practicable. Julia hastily bathed little Alice's swollen and red eyes, and brushed down her rumpled hair; then without a look in the glass on her own account, took the only half-soothed child by the hand and followed the crowd downstairs, without a second glance at Louie.

Miss Barlow had taken advantage of the summons to dinner to leave the scene of defeat; for defeated she had been, having sacrificed her dignity to her temper, and being got the better of by her luckier and cooler pupil; and soon the room was left to her alone, Addy McFarlane being the last to go down. She lingered as long as possible, longing to say something that would mar the pleasure of her antagonist's holiday, something that would prick and fret her through all the excitement and amusement that was in store for her. But for once the failed; the shafts of her malice fell off harmlessly from the elastic good humor, that even the episode of splash and squall had not permanently deranged; and she had to swallow her chagrin as best she might, when, ten minutes later, she saw a flutter of pink muslin pass the dining-room windows, and knew that Louie was safely and happily off on the most delightful of all possible larks, with not a thought of "the girls she left behind her;" nor with any thought, in point of fact, that was not colored by the hope and tenderness and affection that for the time surrounded her.

CHAPTER V.

"Oh, to what uses shall we put
   The wild weed-flower that simply blows?
And is there any moral shut
   Within the bosom of the rose?

"But any man that walks the mead
   In bud or bloom or blade may find,
According as his humors lead,
   A meaning suited to his mind."

               TENNYSON.

HOLIDAYS! Schoolgirls, make the most of them: there's nothing in after years that bears any analogy to them, nothing that answers to them in freshness of enjoyment and intensity of excitement. The feel of one's best clothes on a common "worky day," the thought that flashes through to make all brighter by comparison, "what I was doing this time yesterday;" the meeting with people unassociated with marks and misconduct; the seeing articles of furniture in no way allied in design or application to desks or blackboards; the doing what

72

none of the rest are doing, a happiness in itself; the liberty of speech and action, sudden and intoxicating; the entire freedom from care and responsibility, the utter license anticipation has, the wild strides imagination takes; all these things you have enjoyed and are enjoying now, perhaps, but they will cease when the dull routine of your school life ceases, they will have an end as soon as your daily discipline has an end. You earn, in a sort of way, those bright little gaps in your existence; only those who work know the luxury of rest; you work now, whether against your will or with it, and so you are allowed to feel the sweets of relaxation.

But too many of you will feel those sweets for the last time when you turn your back on school; too many of you mean and hope to have done with work when you have done with school, to make it all one long holiday, all relaxation and delight. *Ah, pauvrettes!* That cannot be; things are fixed inevitably to thwart you there. It is only work that can win the reward of rest; duty done, that can be crowned with peace; pleasures renounced, that will come back to you real pleasures. "There may be a cloud without a rainbow, but there cannot be a rainbow without a cloud." There may be work without reward, but there is not often reward without work.

4

It was the loveliest possible June afternoon, and everything, in Louie's eyes, from the sky overhead to the grass under foot, looked holiday-fashion, and ten times brighter than they had ever looked before, or ever would again for her, perhaps, poor little beginner in a world of trouble.

"Louie, walk, don't fly," called out Tom, in distress. "I never saw anything like the pace at which you and Uncle Rawdon are going."

In fact, it was a very difficult thing for Louie to walk moderately, or talk moderately, or do anything reasonably; and Col. Ruthven, always watching her changeable face, to please her without letting her know his object, had said as they descended the Hall steps:

"Let Tom and his mother saunter along at their usual pace; we will hurry on and order dinner. Tom's legs are too short to take him over the ground very fast, you see."

At this Tom was very irate, and challenged Louie to a race without further preliminaries; but the colonel said it was unconstitutional, gave his arm to Louie, and left Tom to his fate and his mamma; and the result was, they were in the little parlor at the hotel before the latter hove in sight around the corner of Main street.

"Take off your bonnet, Louie," said Col. Ruthven, ringing for dinner, "and do not look so intensely excited. I shall be afraid to come for you again if you don't learn to take holidays more philosophically. Why, child, how your cheeks burn. Tell me, are you quite well?"

"Quite—oh, yes!" she answered, moving restlessly about the room, looking out of the windows and into the plaster vases on the mantelpiece, and turning over the leaves of the books on the table. "I'm well now. I've had a headache for ever so long, but it's all gone since you came for me. Indeed, sir, I'll be as philosophical as you wish, only don't say I shan't have any more holidays. They're the only things I look forward to with the smallest pleasure. All the rest is hateful."

"That's not as it ought to be, Louie; I hoped to have found you contented and happy, but I knew you were the reverse from the moment I saw you. What is it? Can you not tell me?"

But at this moment, the noisy advent of Tom threw the party into some confusion, and excited many remonstrances from all; then dinner was brought up—such a nice, hot little dinner, with an immense preponderance of dessert, great varieties of tarts, and cakes, and puddings, and a pyramid of ice-cream, all, of course, out of compliment to school-girl taste, for Mrs. Appleton was a dyspeptic, and never touched any after-dinner vanities, and the colonel seemed to have no very great appreciation of them; so there was a vast amount of work to be done by the juveniles. Tom certainly did not shirk his duty, but Louie, though she fancied she wanted everything, and was in an ecstasy at every new delicacy, was far too much excited to eat.

"Alas! that eyes like thine
Should sparkle at an apple-pie!"

cried Tom, in a brief, unemployed interval before his plate came back.

"Alas! that they should 'take it out in sparkling,'" said the colonel. "Louie, you're a little hypocrite. You have eaten nothing."

"Oh, sir, did you mean me to? For you've kept me so busy laughing, there hasn't been any time to do it in."

"He'd have given an intermission if you'd asked him. Five minutes between each joke; wouldn't you, Uncle Rawdon?"

"I should have needed fifteen after the Scotch gentleman at the *café*. Oh, I shall make great capital of that when I go back to school; I'll make the girls shout over it some night before Miss Barlow comes upstairs. Miss Barlow hates to hear us

.augh; she thinks she 'smells a mice' if anybody titters."

"She's not far wrong, ordinarily, I'm afraid," said the colonel, laughing. "If school-girls are at all analogous to school-boys, there is good cause for apprehension to an unenlightened party when a titter occurs."

"Oh! I assure you, we don't dare to poke fun at Miss Barlow. She's far too sharp for that. Though everybody in the dormitory hates her, they all mind, after a fashion, and she keeps sublime order."

"Ah, Louie," said Mrs. Appleton, "I'm afraid you are growing a little rebellious. I hope you are not getting to think with too many school-children, that your teachers are your natural enemies. That's a too common mistake, and makes the relation doubly hard to both."

"No, indeed," cried Louie, warmly. "Dear Mrs. Appleton, I hope you don't think that of me. I don't hate all my teachers by any means. I love Miss Stanton dearly, and the Matron is as good as she can be, and Mr. Rogers, and Miss Emily, and Miss Wells, I like extremely; even Miss Marbais, though she's strict and sharp, is just and sensible, and don't do anything for spite, and I don't have any trouble in getting along with her; but Miss Barlow is so mean and so ugly, that I can't help it,

but I do detest the very sight of her. Don't look
so, ·dear Mrs. Appleton! I know its wicked,
but "——

" 'It is your nature' to," put in Tom, very much
afraid of the conversation taking a moral turn, in
which event he was sure of getting many bruises.
"By the way, how's your friend, the McFarlane?"

"Finely, thank you; a degree fonder of me than
ever. But, oh! let me tell you how beautifully I
used her up in French class to-day."

"Do," said Tom with great interest. And Louie,
with much *naïveté*, but considerable cleverness and
spirit, proceeded to recount the little stratagem already mentioned, by which she had appropriately
rewarded Adelaide McFarlane's "meanness;" and
her audience, sorely against their consciences,
laughed an involuntary applause. Sweet Mrs.
Appleton thought it was dreadfully naughty, and
put her cambric handkerchief before her face, hoping that nobody would see how much it diverted
her, while the colonel, after a short, amused laugh,
looked down at the young sinner with a grave
shake of the head but a droll sparkle of the eye.
Louie had a secret but comfortable conviction that,
no matter what enormities she might have been engaged in, Col. Ruthven was and would be her
friend through them all. Tom was vociferous in

his applause; he had to go away from the table, and throw himself on the sofa, rolling over and over in a state of uncontrollable entertainment.

He was only roused from it when the subject of the afternoon's amusement was brought up for discussion; the question, shall we send for a carriage and take a drive, or go for a boat and take a row, had considerable interest for him. He knew if the latter plan prevailed, his uncle would insist upon his taking an oar, and Tom by nature was averse to exertion; so he pricked up his ears, and said cutely as soon as the suggestions were made:

"Louie hates boating; I think she'd enjoy a drive more. Wouldn't you, Louie?"

"Oh, I've no preferences," said Louie, mischievously. "If it will be any disappointment to you to give up rowing, I think we'd better go, by all means."

"I have no doubt you would each enjoy going the way you didn't want to, to spite the other, but I shall not indulge you this time. Madame shall have the casting vote; *voyons*, shall we drive or sail?"

Mrs. Appleton, who had a secret terror of the water, of course inclined to the drive, so in twenty minutes a carriage was at the door, and the whole party were disposing of themselves in it. It was a

phaeton, and Col. Ruthven proposed driving, and
suggested to Louie to take the seat by him in front.
Tom was quite jealous and chagrined, he had
aspired to that honor himself; and after they were
started, Louie said, low, to Col. Ruthven, "Perhaps I'd better give the seat to Tom, I think he's
disappointed."

"Nonsense, Tom rides beside me every day, he
may very well afford to sit on the back seat like a
gentleman, once in a while. Besides, *I* should be
disappointed if you changed your place, so you'd
have to be distressed either way."

"Well then, sir, I think I'll let Tom be disappointed. He gets over it, I know, for I've often
seen him, but I don't know how it might affect you
—I never saw you disappointed."

"I hope you never may, Louie."

"Oh, Tom!" cried Louie, looking back. "Isn't
this splendid! Ar'nt we going fast!"

"Fast!" responded that *blasé* lad, contemptuously.
"I am astonished at you, Louisa. A girl who has
ridden time and again behind my uncle Rawdon's
bays, to say such a thing as that, is perfectly dis-
heartening, perfectly! Why, my dear child, we
are crawling, positively, nothing more. Those old
beasts couldn't get off a walk if they tried."

"That's all spite and envy because you're not

driving yourself. Tom, I blush for you. We are passing everything on the road, if we ar'nt off a walk."

"Yes, all the fences and trees. Oh, Uncle Rawdon, do drive round by the Hall! I want to get a glimpse at the McFarlane; Louie says this is the hour the girls are all on the bank, and it's a good chance. Besides, she and I agreed it would be so nice to dash past the house, and make all the girls die of envy."

"Now, Tom!" cried Louie in an agony of blushing, "you ought to be ashamed to say so."

That some such confidence had passed between them however was pretty clear, since an entirely unfounded charge could hardly have produced such an excessive embarrassment; but Louie begged Col. Ruthven so earnestly to drive the other way, that he could not but comply. She soon forgot all about her embarrassment, however, and the folly of exciting envy, and the vanity of triumph, when they reached the open fields and the rich June-crowned woods of the neighboring country. It was so sweet, so fresh, so peaceful, the erring, willful, discontented, child was for the moment soothed into quiet reverence and gratitude.

"Oh, if such evenings as this would always last," she exclaimed involuntarily, as they drove home-

4*

ward, the rosy sunset slowly fading out of the sky,
" it wouldn't be so hard to be good."

" ' But patience ; there may come a time,' " said
the low voice of her godmother.

"Is it wrong to wish for it, I wonder ?" but Louie
said it in so low a tone none but her companion
caught the words.

" Wish for what, child ?"

" For the end of trouble, and trying, and vexation
and sin."

" My child, God will send the end when He sees
we are perfected."

Col. Ruthven looked for a moment earnestly and
anxiously at his young companion ; her tone had
been so strange, low as it was, that it startled him ;
her lips were compressed, and her dark eyes had a
momentary look of suffering that he had never seen
in them before.   But it was only momentary ;
before he could put his solicitude into words, the
cloud was gone, and with more zest than ever, she
was laughing with Tom, the color again in her face
and the animation in her eye.

Only once again that evening he noticed the same
look. Mrs. Appleton had gone to her room immediately after tea, ill with a headache, and while his
uncle had gone down to smoke, Tom had under-
taken to entertain the young guest. He had repre-

sented to her the attractiveness of the balcony, and as Louie was, according to him, eminently a girl always ready to do what you asked her, of course she acceded to his proposal to sit there. It was very attractive, certainly; the moon was full, and the night serene, and through a gap in the trees there was a glimpse of the river, with the moon making a path of glory along it. But though it was an attractive, it was anything but a prudent situation for the two children, heated with a series of waltzes that had succeeded the tea, and with no other covering to Louie's bare shoulders than her white muslin mantilla, and with that damp breeze coming across the river. It was very imprudent, but Louie never thought of that, and she sat leaning against the iron railing, with Tom sitting at her feet on the sill of the French window, chatting harmlessly and childlishly for a long, long while.

But this had been a day of great length and some exertion to Tom, and this was an unusual hour for him to be still out of bed, and by and by Louie was not surprised to find that his active tongue flagged, and a sort of incoherency and debility crept into his usually terse, nervous style of language, and his brisk sentences degenerated into disjointed and unmeaning attempts to prove he was perfectly wide awake, and finally ceased altogether, and he slept.

When Col. Ruthven, half an hour later, came up-stairs, he found his little nephew asleep with his head on the sill of the window, and Louie, unmoved from her first attitude, leaning against the iron rail-ing with her chin on her clasped hands, looking intently across the shining river. He was startled again as he saw that almost fierce look in her eyes; she was pale, and her white drapery and the white moonlight made him wonder almost if this were the same child he had left an hour ago, so rosy and happy and careless.

"Louie!" he exclaimed, almost angrily, "what are you doing? You have not surely been sitting out there since I left you? I could not have believed you could have been so imprudent."

After he had roused Tom, however, and brought them in, he was surer than ever that she had done an imprudent thing; her lips were purple, and cold shivering chills crept over her, making her teeth chatter in a tell-tale way. He brought her a warm shawl and wrapped her in it, and rang for his sis-ter's maid to take her to her room, parting with her with many injunctions to go immediately to bed, and to see that she had plenty of blankets to keep her warm.

Letty, the maid, was not a very experienced person, and her offers of assistance were not particularly urgent, so Louie soon dismissed her, preferring to undress herself. Letty reappeared, however, after a few minutes, with a glass of something very hot and sweet and strong, that the colonel had sent her to take. She thanked Letty and desired her to thank the colonel, bolted the door after her, put her lips to the glass, turned up her nose very disgustedly and set the glass on the mantelpiece in an entirely undiminished state, where it stayed till the chambermaid took it away in the morning.

That night was a very wretched one to Louie. Whatever had been her troubles before, she had always been able to get rid of them at night, and though she might have cried herself to sleep, slept none the less soundly for it. But now she crept shivering and cold to bed, and for a long while lay awake, shaking with chills. Then she fell into a sort of uneasy doze, from which she waked soon, burning hot, smothering with the blankets, stifling for want of air; and from that time till morning, tossed from side to side of the wide bed, uncomfortable every way, more restless and wretched than she had ever been before.

Would morning never come? would those cold stars never go away, shining so fixedly at her through the small panes of the window below the bed! would there never be any stir in the house again! it was so dismally still! such a headache, and such miserable homesick thoughts as came with it; and such a dull aching in all her limbs! But the longest night must have an end, and even this one terminated at last, and a cold grey dawn succeeded it, during which she found a short repose, from which Letty unfeelingly aroused her about seven o'clock.

When Louie came into the breakfast-room, no one would have guessed the sort of night she had spent; she had such a bright color, and her lips were so red, that the heaviness of her eyes and the unsteadiness of her hand passed unnoticed. She rather evaded the breakfast question, playing with her knife and fork a good deal more than she used them; but then that was nothing very unusual with her; excitement invariably took all her appetite away. Tom, indeed, seemed much the greater sufferer from the evening's folly, having an unmistakable attack of the "snuffles," and looking very stupid and forlorn. They were never to be trusted again, the colonel said. Tom should have a nurse to look after him, and Louie must never again be out of Miss Barlow's sight.

"I don't know which would be the most to be

pitied in that case, Miss Barlow or me," said Louie, laughing.

"I know," cried Tom, maliciously, "Miss Barlow would be the worst off by great odds."

"Oh, she would, would she? Then we can't even speculate upon the wretched state of the nurse Col. Ruthven promises you. I'm sure, Tom, I pity *her* from my heart, if you're always as cross when you're waked as you were last night."

"But I'm not; you're not always by, you know, and in the absence of any provoking cause, I am good-natured, everybody allows. Now, that's enough for once, Louisa; please to hand me a muffin."

"A buffin," repeated the young lady, handing him the plate.

"Uncle Rawdon, speak to her, it interferes with my digestion to be annoyed at meal-time."

Small Tom was such a parrot, and used so ludicrously the phrases and mannerisms of his elders, that no one could help smiling at his impertinences. He was clever and sensible, too, with all his spoiled-child ways, and though he had never known anything in his life but indulgence, and was shrewd enough to see that he was the most important member of the family circle, and could in ordinary cases carry everything before him, he did not abuse his power very much, but contented himself with hav-

ing his own way quietly, and enjoying moderately
what would have been the ruin of almost any other
boy.   He was far too clever not to see that his
mother had no other object in life than his advance-
ment and advantage, and that he was his uncle
Rawdon's pride and darling; that he had more
money now than any other boy he knew, and would
have, when he was a man, more than most men
have; but to save him from being spoiled by all this,
he had been blessed with a more than ordinary
share of sterling good sense and sobriety; he was
one of those children who seem born with good
principles, self-reliant and steady from their baby-
hood, and who never go very far wrong in the outward conduct of their lives, at least.

The temptations of such are very subtile, and lie
so far below the surface, that they are often harder
to combat than the volatile passions of more impul-
sive natures.   Self-reliance may grow into self-con-
fidence; steady aims are not always high aims:
hardihood and resolution, if they are not Christian-
ized, may prove snares and impediments in the way
of life, may harden and stunt the character and stop
its healthy growth.   It is very difficult for a man who
finds by experience that he is wiser and discreeter
than his neighbors, to preserve that humility that is
necessary to make his goodness acceptable with

God. It is very difficult, and nothing but the grace of that God can keep him from the most hopeless of all states, the state of a hard, cold, self-satisfied man of the world, irreproachably moral, hopelessly irreligious.

But it isn't best to go into mourning for poor little Tom yet; he is but a tiny lad, and though he has, in that sharp, shrewd, sensible brain and unenthusiastic temperament the germs of such a fate, they may not ripen into evil; God's grace, won by his mother's prayers, and fostered by her love and daily teaching, may overshadow and overcome them. Besides, he has before him in his uncle, an example that may well stir his admiration, and being as far as it is possible for him to be, impressed with a desire to copy it, perhaps he may succeed. He is a child of few admirations, few friendships, but he loves mamma, admires Uncle Rawdon, and and is absolutely fond of Louie; and as they are all safe and proper objects of affection, possibly they may do much toward making him the sort of boy they'd like to see him.

"I'm jealous of you, Lou," he said, sauntering up to the sofa where that young lady sat bending over a sketch-book of Col. Ruthven's, while its owner, standing beside the window, smoked a fragrant Havana, or leaning forward pointed out to her the

charms of different views, and explained the odd
sounding long foreign names below them. "I verily
believe Uncle Rawdon cares as much for you as he
does for me."

"As much!" cried Louie, throwing up her eyes.
"I shouldn't be contented if I didn't think he liked
me twice as well. Don't you now, sir? Please say
yes!"

Col. Ruthven looked down at her; though she
was very arch and laughing and looked prettier
than usual, the question did not seem to please him,
however the face might: after a moment's scrutiny
of it, too frank and childish not to be read through
at a glance, he averted his own with something between a sigh and a gesture of impatience, and said
carelessly as he moved away.

"What do such children as you know of degrees
of liking? Tops and kites will keep Tom's heart,
and sugar-plums will win Louie's for a good many
years yet. That's the affection you have to give,
n'est ce pas, mes petits?"

But they did not have time or opportunity to
resent the suggestion; the door closed behind the
speaker and they were left alone. Tom took some
time to digest the idea, while Louie thoughtfully
turned the leaves of the sketch-book.

"That was mean of Uncle Rawdon," said the

youth at length, with considerable energy. "I *don't* like him for his tops and kites. I'd put all he ever gave me in the fire, if I thought he was in earnest. I never liked anybody yet for what they gave me. Uncle Richard gives me as many things as Uncle Rawdon, and I don't care *that* for him, and don't pretend to, either. I say, Louie, you don't think he meant it?"

"No, oh no! he couldn't, something must have vexed him or he meant to tease us. Perhaps he didn't like my asking him that; perhaps it sounded saucy—I'm very sorry."

"He oughtn't to complain of our being saucy, while he spoils us so. Why he pets you to death, and lets you say and do just as you choose, always, and likes of all things to have you droll and pert. No it couldn't have been that—Hang! I hate to have him out with me. I think I care more for him than for anybody else. He's such a brick, Louie! He's such a sort of a man that it makes you feel mean to have him think you're mean, even for a minute. What wouldn't I give to be like him when I'm grown up! To make people afraid of me without any fuss and bluster, and to be so manly and so clever and so quiet. Do you know, I think he's the finest gentleman I ever saw?"

"Except the Bishop," said Louie, thoughtfully.

"Well, yes, except the Bishop, I suppose. Uncle Rawdon says himself the Bishop is the most elegant man he knows, and I'm sure he ought to know. It must be very fine to be that sort of a gentleman, a gentleman all the way through—no pretence, no make believe, no grand airs; the very carmen in the streets could tell the difference between a gentleman that wanted to be thought a gentleman, and a gentleman that never thought anything about it, but was just himself, just involuntary, just outside as he was in his own heart."

"Children! are you ready to take a walk with me?" called out Mrs. Appleton from the other room.

Louie said, "Yes ma'am," rising slowly, and Tom put away the sketch-book for her with more considerateness than usual.

It was such a sweet summer morning that the walk, though rather listlessly begun, soon proved a pleasure. There was just animation enough in the streets of the quiet old town to amuse the children, while Mrs. Appleton stopped for the replenishment of Louie's very hardly used and unenduring wardrobe, and the hours slipped quickly away. There were but two more left of Louie's holiday, her heart told her, with a pang, as the clock struck eleven—but two hours more of pleasure left.

CHAPTER VI.

ASHES OF ROSES.

" Nae treasures, nor pleasures,
    Can make us happy lang;
The *heart* aye's the part aye,
    That makes us right or wrang."

BURNS.

"WHERE can Uncle Rawdon be all this time?" said Tom discontentedly, as they came out of the shoemaker's on the corner. "It's taken him a monstrous while to smoke that cigar.—Ah! there he comes up the street. He's motioning us to stop; wait a minute, mamma," as Mrs. Appleton was turning down a cross street on the way to the dressmaker's.

"Where are you going?" asked Col. Ruthven, joining them on the corner.

"Why, Louie tells me she has no dress nice enough to wear to the Bishop's on the Fourth, and I've just being getting her a white muslin, and we are on our way to the dressmaker's to have it fitted. We've not much time to spare either, I fear."

"It's just eleven," said the gentleman looking at his watch. "If your artist does not keep you long, we may have time for a drive before lunch. Would you like it, Louie?"

"Yes, sir, thank you," she returned timidly and with some confusion, not quite certain whether she was restored to the favor she had so innocently and inadvertently lost an hour before. He saw her embarrassment and looking down kindly at her, said with a smile:

"It's hardly matter for gratitude, I think, at least as yet."

He gave his arm to his sister, and Louie and Tom followed at a little distance. The dressmaker lived in a little square box of a white house, with vividly green blinds and a little square green yard in front of it; Tom said it hurt his eyes, the green and the white were so extremely bright, and he rather grumbled at having to wait and walk up and down outside with his uncle. However, Col. Ruthven treated him to a little longer walk, having no faith in the dressmaker's ten minutes, and they made the tour of Main street and the bank, pausing at more than one shop by the way, and had several minutes to spare waiting by the gate, before the door opened and the ladies were released.

"Well, is she going to make you very fine?"

asked Tom, opening the gate. "I should think she'd been trying on forty dresses, instead of one wretched white muslin, from the time she took."

"I'm sure we haven't been long."

"Of course not; ladies never think they're long when they are pow-wow-ing over a fashion plate with a dressmaker. I always 'settle my brains for a long winter's nap,' when mamma leaves me in the carriage while she just runs into Roumier's, to give an order about the sleeve trimming of a morning dress or some such vanity."

"Tom, I fear you embellish."

"Louie, I don't. Mamma will tell you so herself, it is the way all ladies do, but I'm sorry to find you're getting so young-ladyfied as to do it too. Last year you wouldn't: a whole half hour under the dressmaker's hands!—I wouldn't have been the dressmaker! But now you're beginning to think about fine clothes and looking pretty, and I don't think you're worth as much by a third as you used to be. Uncle Rawdon, don't you think it's tiresome in Louie to grow so much older? I don't think she's half as nice this term."

"Oh, Tom!" cried Louie, half vexed, "how silly you are. I'm sure no girl of my age ever put on less young lady airs; and if I am tiresome, I can't help it. You'd be tiresome, too, if—if"——

"If what, my little girl?" asked Col. Ruthven, kindly.

"If he were as far away from his mother, as I am from mine, and if he had just the sort of a time at school as I have, no pleasures and no holidays—and everything so hateful."

"Oh, nonsense, Louie! you know I didn't mean it."

"Louie, child," said Mrs. Appleton, laying her hand affectionately on the girl's, "I am afraid all's not quite right in your own heart, when everything is hateful. School is a little world, and is pretty cold and hard, sometimes, just like the great world; but to us ourselves, it is very much as we make it. If we choose to be misanthropical, why, we shall see only what is cold and hard and hateful in the people in it; but if we have a real love for goodness and holiness in our hearts, we shall be pretty sure to find out something answering to those feelings in others. And people will treat us according to our treatment of them; we can make an atmosphere of gentleness and charity around us that will affect every one who comes near us; or we can be so perverse and unlovable, that even our best friends will catch the contagion and will be repulsive in their turn. Don't think I mean to lecture you, my little god-daughter; I wouldn't for the world, seem unkind; but you know I am too fond of you to bear to see you out of the way of being happy, and your dear mother left you, in a sort of way, to my protection. What should I say to her, if she should come back and find her little Louie, whom she left so docile and affectionate, a discontented, imperious, impatient girl? How could I excuse myself for not having run the risk of doing a little disagreeable ' lecturing?' "

There are not many girls who can understand what it was that made Louie start so nervously and repulse the affection that she was longing to receive, so shortly; there are not many, perhaps, but there are some who can understand the rush of feeling that her mother's name brought, the agony of unhappiness and tenderness, and yet the keen shame of betraying her emotion, the dread of crying before Col. Ruthven, and of making Tom laugh at her, as laugh he surely would; in a moment more she would have done it—catching her breath and looking away, she said quickly, and with an unnaturally cold laugh:

"Oh, mother won't blame you; she knows I'm very bad, she knows lectures don't do me any good."

"I wish lectures could be abolished by act of Congress," cried Tom. "They're pernicious in

their tendencies; they've done me an immense
amount of harm."

Mrs. Appleton sighed low and humbly, while the
others laughed; it was strange, how cold and perverse the two children, whom she loved most, were.
She hardly knew how to reach them; Louie, certainly, she failed to comprehend; at once affectionate and repulsing affection, warm-hearted, yet perverse and trifling. Five minutes alone with her
would have solved it; Louie would have given
anything for them; they would have been an unspeakable relief to Mrs. Appleton, but they never
came.

"The tender grace of a day that was dead,"

Eternity could alone make up to them.

"Ah!" cried Tom, "good bye to our drive!
There's company in the parlor. Why *will* people
come when they're not wanted!"

"That's a question that has puzzled older heads
than yours," said the colonel, *sotto voce.* He did
not seem any more pleased than his nephew, to
find their little parlor invaded by visitors, and to
have to spend the last hour of his young favorite's
holiday, in saying polite commonplaces to people
he did not care at all for, and had not seen for
months, and did not wish to see for months
to come. For he did care for Louie, it was

not hard to see, and would rather have watched her changeable face, and listened to her naïve chat, than have talked to a roomful of the most intellectual ladies and gentlemen our country has yet produced. It was very odd and inexplicable, but the wisest people sometimes take odd and inexplicable fancies, and it was with a look of much relief and pleasure, that he returned from putting the ladies in their carriage, to the parlor, where the children by the window, and Mrs. Appleton on the sofa, rested after the fatigues of the morning.

"Uncle, I've rung for lunch," Master Tom said. "We are hungry as savages, and Louie'll have barely time to eat it and get back to the Hall, before time for the train to start."

"Well, urchin, I know that."

Lunch was by no means the gayest of the four meals they had taken in that pleasant little parlor. Tom's spirits, indeed, were unabated, but Mrs. Appleton had a headache, and could not stay it half out, returning to lie on the sofa, while the colonel, though he talked enough, was none too gay, and Louie could only feel as if a weight of lead were lying at her heart, growing heavier and harder every minute. Long before Tom had thought of being through his *rôle*, however, Col. Ruthven, looking at his watch, said:

"I am afraid, Louie, it is time for you to put your bonnet on."

"Yes, sir," she said, getting up from the table, with a very miserable, homesick realization of having "come to the end of her rope." How differently she felt as she tied the pink bonnet strings under her chin, from yesterday afternoon as she tied them. They should have been ashes of roses in color to-day, instead of roses, to have matched her feelings.

"Tom, you can't leave your lunch to walk back with us, I suppose. Well, good bye, then. Am I to kiss you?"

"I think you may. You're a good fellow, Louie, if you are a girl. You may write to me, too, next week. Uncle Rawdon will give you the address."

"Yes, Louie dear, you must write often," said Mrs. Appleton, raising herself from the sofa. "We shall want to hear from you constantly."

"I am sorry to hurry you, my dear Louie, but we must be off. One more kiss and your god-mamma must let you go. Carry, you will be ready by the time I return from the Hall? There will be no more than time to get to the depot."

"Yes, Letty has packed the valises; I have nothing but to put my bonnet on—good bye, my darling."

What Tom's last six sentences were, or what her own responses pretended to be, Louie would have found it difficult to have told ; they were some distance on their way before she found voice to answer any of her companion's questions, or composure to think quietly and reasonably about anything.

Col. Ruthven was too kind to need any excuse for her silence, and left her quiet for a little while, then said in a low tone as he took her hand, " Why what a silly child this is! You surely have forgotten how soon the summer will pass, and how soon that glorious October vacation will be here!"

Louie shook her head as she struggled to keep back the tears.

"It will be soon enough no doubt, sir, to you all, but to me it will be ages and ages "——

"Now, Louie, my sensible little girl! I am ashamed of you. I thought you were wiser. Last spring when you came back you promised not to be homesick ; you told me you had outgrown such follies."

"I know—but it was different then. I didn't mind things half so much. Oh, I wish you'd write to papa and ask him if I need stay any longer : Papa does everything you want always—won't you, dear Col. Ruthven ?"

"Why, what should I tell him, little one? That you had changed your mind and concluded not to like school any more? That the McFarlane teased you, or the Barlow wouldn't let you laugh? No no, my dear little girl, I know your own good heart will tell you something much better than that. It will tell you to be háppy where it is your duty to be, and to be patient and strong under your little trials. They are not little? Oh! yes, *petite*, they are. Wait till you have tasted real ones; you will see how slight they are, what summer breezes they are compared with the tempests that life will bring you. Bear them bravely, look at them honestly and sensibly, and you will soon master yourself and them. I know you well enough to know that you will soon be happier and wiser. I trust to your own good sense to recover you from your present discontent; it's very natural, my dear Louie, very natural, but nevertheless, very unsafe. Indifference to present duties, and repining for forbidden pleasures, though they are temptations that we can never quite shake off, are particularly dangerous to one whose character is just forming, and at a time when every emotion *tells* upon its formation, through life perhaps. And you must promise me, Louie, that you will try to get the better of them—promise me that you will try to be happy and patient."

"I'll try to be patient—I can't promise to be happy."

"If you are one, the other will come; I am not afraid—ah! here we are at the Hall! I have so much more to say, I am sorry our walk is at an end. Forgive the lecture, Louie. You have had so much lecturing I am afraid it has spoiled your holiday."

"Ah no! I don't mind such lectures—I wish I could have them every day."

"Write to us very often, Louie, once a week at the very longest."

"Yes, sir."

Louie sighed as they ascended the steps; Col. Ruthven paused a moment at the door, and putting a little package in her hand, said, "There are some ribbons, Louie, for that white dress; think of this pleasant holiday and me when you wear them, and don't disgrace them or the memory, by a want of smiles. Just fancy I'm looking over your shoulder every time you put them on before the glass, and am looking very stern whenever the face I see there is pale and dismal—when it is a face at all, in fact, like the one I see now."

"I can't always help my face," said Louie, struggling to get up a smile, "but you're so kind, I'll try to get my heart better. Don't think, sir, I'm not grateful."

"For what, my little friend?——Good bye!"

"Good bye, sir," faltered Louie.

"God bless you!"

He hurried down the steps; Louie watched him out of sight, and then with a weary sigh, shut the door upon her ended holiday, reality and work and discipline in the very atmosphere of the place as she entered it.

CHAPTER VII.

LOUIE'S LATINITY.

"A girl, who has so many willful ways
  She would have caused Job's patience to forsake him;
Yet is so rich in all that's girlhood's praise,
Did Job himself upon her goodness gaze,
  A little better she would surely make him."

CERTAINLY, holidays are unprofitable things, miserable, unsettling, unsatisfactory things; and Louie thought, as she sat down on the side of her bed, slowly taking off her holiday clothes, she almost wished she had not had one. It was hardly worth the pain of coming back to every-day life again, and finding it so wretchedly insipid after the exhilarating draught; it was almost worse than no pleasure at all, this dead pleasure. What good did it do her that she had been so happy yesterday? No good; only made to-day darker by comparison; only made present duties doubly irksome.

Her toilette took far more time than it had taken yesterday; though it was only a calico frock to be hooked on, and a linen collar to be pinned with

the little coral pin Col. Ruthven sent at Christmas, it
was a long time in being accomplished. There was
a languor and indifference about her movements that
contrasted strongly with the spirit of yesterday's
dressing. And when it was all done, the pink muslin, with a heartfelt sigh, restored to its peg in the
wardrobe, the little straw hat shut into its box, the
white mantilla folded and laid on its shelf, she felt
much more like lying down on the bed and having
a good cry, than going downstairs to work and study
among all those busy, careless girls, who knew so little how she felt, and cared so little for her feelings.

She was on her knees before her trunk, putting
away the dear little package of ribbon, and wondering whether she should ever have the heart to
wear it, when the door suddenly opened, and Alice
Aulay put her head in the room.

"Mr. Van Buren says come right down to your
Latin."

"How did Mr. Van Buren know I'd come back,
pray?" asked Louie, sharply.

"Addy McFarlane told him you had, when the
class went down to him; she was practising in the
dining-room and saw you go up the steps. You'd
better hurry."

"I haven't the least intention of hurrying," returned Louie, slowly closing and locking her trunk.

Now, Alice, though in the main a well-disposed little girl, had yet some love of mischief-making and perverseness in her; the quarrel of yesterday still rankled in her mind; besides, she had been sent upstairs with the message much against her will, and felt a grudge against Louie as the cause; so she very naturally and very naughtily went back to Mr. Van Buren's class, and said, opening the door wide enough to get her yellow curls in:

"I told Louie to come, sir, and that you said she must hurry, but she said she wouldn't hurry, and she was mad because I came."

Mr. Van Buren, who was a nervous little old man, started and looked very much as if he wanted to box somebody's ears, and demanded wrathfully, "if Miss Atterbury had sent him word she wouldn't hurry?"

"Why, I don't know, sir," said the child, beginning to get frightened, "whether she sent word or no; she said she wouldn't, though—she said she hadn't any intention of hurrying."

"That's another part of speech," returned the professor, cooling down somewhat. "How came you, little girl, to return to me as if you had been sent with that message? I don't like it; I don't think it looks honest. I think you deserve a punishment."

Alice, who knew very little of professors, and

stood in great awe of them, turned very pale at
this, and looked ready to cry, and stood twisting
the handle of the door very nervously, uncertain
whether to go or stay—whether Mr. Van Buren
had done scolding her, or whether he had just
begun—when Louie, with a lagging step and very
listless air, made her appearance.

"Well, Miss Atterbury"—began the old gentleman, with whom Louie had always been rather a
favorite, and who was in consequence doubly irritated at her misdemeanor—"well, Miss Atterbury, I am glad to find you have not altogether
renounced my class. I shall be under the neces-
sity of renouncing you as a member of it, if I ever
receive such an answer to my summons from you
again."

"I don't understand what you mean, sir," she returned, surprised and angry.

"I mean, when I desire you to hurry, you are
never to send me word again, you have no intention of hurrying."

"I did not send you any such word, sir."

"At any rate, you said as much, whether you
sent any such word or not. I shall remember it,
young lady, in my future estimation of you. I
shall remember that you can be at once disrespectful and indolent."

Alice, who, during this parley, had been shaking with terror, had crept for protection to the side of her friend, Julia, who sat at the end of the bench nearest to the door, and, clinging to her dress, turned her face away, and did not raise her guilty blue eyes from the floor. Though Julia was extremely vexed at her pet's delinquency, and intended to show her her very great disapprobation of it when they were by themselves, she had not the heart to turn against her now, nor deny the shaking little culprit the asylum she had sought.

How Louie's dark eyes blazed as they swept the group! Julia half pushed Alice away as she met them; then, ashamed of the momentary cowardice, put her arm around her and drew her back. Louie's lips moved, but she did not speak. Mr. Van Buren motioned her to take her seat; then, turning to the little girl, said:

"You may go, little miss. I shall not punish you any further for your dishonesty of purpose and love of mischief; you are too young, perhaps, to understand how wrong your conduct has been, but you are not too young to know that if it is repeated it will gain a punishment for you. You have exposed another's faults at the expense of committing one yourself. Go now. Young ladies, we will proceed with our lesson, too long delayed already by Miss Atterbury's impertinence and Miss Aulay's misrepresentation."

The general respect for Louie's Latinity, it is to be feared, suffered some diminution during this recitation. She had not prepared the lesson, of course, but if she had, it is very doubtful whether, in the tumult of bitter feelings that filled her mind, she could have commanded any recollection of it. Indeed, she failed not only in the prescribed lesson, but in the review which Mr. Van Buren, principally for her benefit, subjected them to. He had always been proud of her proficiency, and secretly looked upon her as the highest trump in his hand, and his chagrin and irritation at her blunders on this occasion were in exact ratio to the hopes he had entertained of making her a first-rate scholar. Before the hour of recitation was over, all the others had dropped into the background, and the luckless Louie alone was paraded before the audience, too excited and angry to do anything but disgrace herself, and making Mr. Van Buren, of course, more excited and angry at every fresh blunder. But he had determined she should construe a passage for him that he was certain she was as familiar with as he was himself, and as much for her own credit with the class as for his own satisfaction, he peremptorily insisted on its accomplishment, till he very nearly lost his own temper in the trial.

Now, though Louie was angry with Mr. Van Buren, angry with Alice, unspeakably angry with Julia, she was not rebellious enough to have refused to do what was required of her, if it had been in her power to do it; but the truth was, her head ached to a bewildering degree—such a degree that the more she tried to think the more she couldn't—the more she tried to grasp a thought or a word the further it seemed to slip away from her, till it was lost in the bewildering maze of other lost thoughts and words; and exactly as Mr. Van Buren's vehemence and determination increased, her self-possession and intelligence decreased, till the scene was wound up by a burst of tears on her part, and a most unqualified reprimand on the part of her teacher.

"I give you five minutes," he concluded, looking at his watch, "to construe that passage for me; at the end of that time, if you cannot or will not do it, you may let Mr. Rogers hear your attempts. I shall be glad to show him what progress you have made."

Of course, at the end of five minutes, Louie was no further ahead than she had been before, indeed, only twice as much confused and hopeless, and, of course, Mr. Van Buren must be as good as his word, and send her to the Study. There was a smothered titter, originating in Addy McFarlane's end of the class, when Louie, with her Virgil in her hand, walked out of the room with burning cheeks and wet eyes, but Mr. Van Buren silenced it angrily.

"You are laughing at a girl," he said, "who till to-day has shown herself so much your superior that I have been unreasonably harsh with her for showing herself for once, on a par with you in stupidity."

The bell rang, and as the class went out, Addy whispered "who was that meant for?" unpleasantly conscious that it was a compliment which she had a perfect right to appropriate.

As for Julia, she had as little heart in the lessons that followed that, as poor Louie had had in her Latin. She could only think of the gesture with which Louie had hidden her face from the stare of her companions, and the burst of tears that had proved the genuineness of her misery; she had never once looked at Julia after that quick glance, the reproach of which Julia tried in vain to get rid of—she had not looked at any one, or seemed to hope for pity from any one. I would give worlds to tell her how sorry I am, thought her friend—

but there was a mountain of coldness and resentment and suspicion between them; what could ever melt it?

The time passed slowly till three o'clock, Louie did not return from the Study. Julia watched the door nervously, expecting her entrance every time it opened. Neither when the bell rang, and all assembled in the schoolroom, did she make her appearance. What could it mean? There was trouble coming, and when Alice ran up to Julia in the entry on their way upstairs, and hid her face in her dress whispering,

"You ar'nt angry with me, Julia dear?"

Julia could only turn away, and say earnestly,

"Yes Alice, more angry than I ever have been with you before. You have made me very unhappy. I can't tell you how unhappy."

Alice began to cry; Julia had never been so unkind before, and much more affected probably by a fear of her displeasure, than by real repentance for her fault, she showed such inconsolable sorrow that at last Julia had to consent to forgive her unconditionally and restore her to favor.

"Where's Lou Atterbury all this while, I wonder?" said Adelaide, as they were preparing for dinner. Julia winced; she dreaded the introduction of that topic almost as much us if it had been her own disgrace, and turning away busied herself in arranging Alice's curls.

"Poor Louie! I wonder indeed," said Laura Boutwell, with a sigh. "She's perpetually in trouble now-a-days. Isn't she in your class, Julia? What happened about her Latin? I heard something of it from Eva Leonard."

"I don't know—I can't tell you exactly."

"Oh, I can," cried Adelaide, officiously; and the episode of Mr. Van Buren succeeded. Laura Boutwell was in senior B. and the oldest girl in the dormitory, quite the queen of it, in fact, and quite worthy of the position, so that Julia felt doubly vexed that she should hear the story of Louie's disgrace from so prejudiced a witness as Adelaide.

"It is too bad," said Laura, thoughtfully. "I don't see what is the matter with Louie—or yes, I do see," she added in a lower tone. "I wish I could help her."

"I wish you could," Julia said in the same voice. "Won't you try to get a chance to talk with her?"

"Yes—I'll try." And Laura's quiet assurance was as good as a dozen promises from anybody else.

Exactly as the dinner bell rang, and while the others were hurrying toward the door, and Julia was twisting hastily the last of the ringlets she had

the charge of, round her finger, Louie entered the
dormitory. There was something about her face
that made a silence for the instant among the chat-
tering girls; they let her pass without a question or
reproach. Julia's heart beat fast; she would have
given anything to have said a single word to her—
in lieu of doing it, she grasped Alice's hand and
hurried out of the room.

At dinner, Eva Leonard, a chatty, clever south-
erner, Louie's nearest neighbor, for once found herself at a loss for subjects of pleasantry. Though
she would have scouted the idea of being afraid of
saying anything she chose to any one, still it was
undeniably the fact that she dropped the sentence
half finished in which she had begun to rally Louie
on her ill-luck, and sank soon into an unusual state
of quiet and thoughtfulness. The utter misery of
her companion's face, hard as she struggled to con-
ceal it, insensibly shocked and subdued her, and
though, as soon as they were released from the table,
she could run out among the others, and whisper
curiously about it, she was quiet enough while
under its influence. Laura Boutwell had been
watching it too, and after dinner, stationing herself
at the door through which Louie must pass, waited
till she came along.

"I've been waiting for you," she said kindly,

joining her. " Will you walk on the bank with me this afternoon ?"

"I can't, thank you," returned Louie in a smothered sort of voice, "I'm not going out to-day," and hurried away.

" Well ?" said Julia, anxiously, as Laura came into the hall alone. Laura shook her head.

" She will not come with me. I am afraid she's very unhappy, and that there's something worse than the Latin in agitation now."

The pleasant afternoon, and the attractions of the bank, did not tempt Julia out that day. She wandered restlessly about the schoolroom and entries, tried first to read, then to study, but failed in doing either ; then went to her hour of practis-ing, glad to have something to do about which she had no choice. At tea, Louie came down late, after grace was said ; Julia glanced up nervously at her, but the glance did not add much to her composure, judging from the untasted meal she left, and the anxious way in which she followed her with her eyes as they left the dining-room.

Study hour had begun; the gas was lit, and the long schoolroom was full of girls, the usual quiet of the hour reigning. Every one studied or pre-tended to study, the scratch of a rapid pen, or the cautious and smothered closing of a desk, alone shocked the silence. Louie was in her seat; since the hour began, she had been sitting with her face shaded by her hand bending over a book that lay before her, but Adelaide's observant eyes had not failed to note, she had not turned a leaf.

The same detective also noted that when the door opened, and some one came down the room to the desk of the teacher in charge, Louie gave a start but did not look up; and when, crossing to where she sat, the teacher touched her on the shoulder and whispered a few words in her ear, and she bowed an assent, it was with a face white as ashes and a hand that shook visibly, that she put up her book and walked out of the room.

" It's coming now !" thought Adelaide, as the door closed after her.

CHAPTER VIII.

THE SKY IS RED AND LOWERING.

" The stubborn knees with holy trembling smite,
  Which bow not at Thine awful name.
Pour from Thine altar Thine own glorious light,
  Winning the world-enamored sight
To turn and see which way the healing radiance came.''
LYRA INNOCENTIUM.

WHEN Louie left the class that afternoon and walked up to the Study door, it would have been a difficult matter to have decided what feelings were strongest in her mind. It seems a severe thing to say of one so childish, so young in evil, but her mobile face expressed two emotions that no face can long express with safety to the soul it interprets— reckless defiance and stubborn hatred. Defiance of the laws that bound her, the restraints that thwarted her, hatred of the injustice that sent her to disgrace, and of the friendship that looked coldly on. But hers was a nature that, as they say, must be either greatly good or greatly evil; strong feelings, that, according to the government they have,

118

are either a blessing or a curse; quick sensibilities, that lead as readily to death as life; a will and a courage that are terrible weapons in the hand of the tempter, if once he gains possession—that are noble and lead to heroism, heavenly, and such as win the martry's crown, if God and good angels have the guidance.

Poor child! Had they the guidance now? Had they had, for many weary months? Months during which she had fretted and rebelled and gone on sinning as persistently as if there were no end to God's patience with those who break His laws; months of carelessness about her soul, disregard of the ordinances of His church, rejection of Confirmation vows, neglect of his Dying Command. Was it strange that the path grew wild and tangled, that darkness and fear were closing her in? It was a path of her own choosing, with guides of her own choosing; no wonder she had gone so far astray.

The look with which Mr. Rogers met her was grave and stern; in any other mood she would have been frightened by its unusual severity, but she was too angry and defiant to be frightened by anything. She received her reproof for the Latin lesson, and its consequent punishment, in sullen silence; rising as Mr. Rogers concluded, she said, "May I go, sir?"

"No," said Mr. Rogers, in a tone of strong displeasure. "No, you may not go. You have paid far too many visits to this room of late, without any manifest improvement to yourself, or satisfaction to me. I shall try to make this one of a nature that will impress itself on your volatile mind, if such impression is possible; I shall hope to make it the last. Louisa, when yesterday morning, you asked permission to write to Miss Barlow instead of speaking to her, you led me to suppose it was because you wished to be respectful and submissive, but doubted your own resolution if obliged to ask pardon in person. I was willing to give you every help in my power, and granted your rather singular request. I now see how much reliance is to be placed on your representations; I have discovered the motive that prompted you to avoid an interview with Miss Barlow. It would have been inconvenient to have explained to her the cause of your long tarry in the school-room; she might have asked what book it was you found so interesting."

"Sir!" said Louie, startled and uncertain. "I do not understand."

"You do not? I am sorry; perhaps I can help you. To begin at the root of the matter, I will ask you what the name of the book was which you went into the school-room to read, and if you answer me honestly, we shall soon see our way through it."

The color in her cheeks paled a little, and her eyes fell beneath Mr. Rogers' stern scrutiny; but the quivering of her mouth, and the uncertain softening of her eyes were all gone, when, at that moment, a low tap at the door made her look up, and when Miss Barlow's small trim figure appeared as it opened. She begged pardon for intruding, but Mr. Rogers requested her to stay and gave her a chair.

"I will repeat," he said, "a question I had just put to Louisa as you entered. What was the book you were reading the other morning when you were late at Chapel?"

Louie's lips moved, she tried to speak, but only grew very pale and turned away.

"I thought it would be a useless question," said Miss Barlow, in a low voice. "Some minds seem incapable of straightforwardness."

The color flashed back into the girl's face and the fire into her eyes.

"You have no right to say that. I never told you a lie in my life, you know I never did, you cannot say I ever did. You have tried your best to frighten me into it, you have never let me alone since I came into your dormitory, and it's

just because I won't lie to you or bend to you or get
out of your way, that you hate me so and tantalize
me so. I don't care what you do to me—I don't
care what happens to me—I won't endure it any
longer—I won't submit to your authority—you
make me ten times worse every time I see you—
you make me so ugly I don't know myself. There
is no use trying to make me mind you. You need
not ask me any questions, for I will not answer
them ; you may spare yourself the trouble of scolding me for I shall not care. You may tell the
Bishop—you may expel me from the school—it
does not matter to me in the very least what
becomes of me."

In the pause that followed these words, you may
well suppose Louie's heart almost stopped beating.
While she had been speaking, the intensity of her
excitement and anger had made her oblivious of
every other consideration ; but now, in the startling
silence that ensued, there came a rush of fear,
shame, terror, that made her turn faint and giddy ;
the room swam before her ; the words she had said,
the words Mr. Rogers began to say, all tangled and
twisted themselves together, and the bewildering
throbbing of her head blotted and blurred them
till they were all one mass of confusion. Mr.
Rogers was speaking—oh! how severely—Miss

Barlow's low but sharp voice mingled with it; what were they talking about—what did it all mean—they seemed to think she understood it all, and to threaten vaguely, punishment for what was worse than vague to her. There was something about a book, and Mr. Rogers took one from his desk, and asked her if she had ever seen it before?

"I don't know," she faltered, as half blind with excitement she bent down to look at it—"not that I remember—no—I don't think I ever have."

A low exclamation of horror fell from Miss Barlow's lips, and Mr. Rogers in a stern voice bade her beware; such cowardly falsehoods could avail her nothing—a simple avowal of her fault was her only chance.

"If I only knew what they meant!" thought the wretched child, pressing her hand involuntarily to her aching temple.

But it soon became evident what they meant, even to her bewildered brain. They meant that, in addition to her other wrong doings, she was accused of breaking the rule that forbade novel read·ing, of being, in fact, the prime cause of all the trouble that had lately existed on account of this same fault among the other girls, of circulating improper books among them, of reading such books as were forbidden at forbidden hours, and of having been found, when sent to her room for a punishment, occupied with the novel now in Mr. Rogers' hands. When at last the whole drift of this became clear to her, she exclaimed indignantly and vehemently :

" It is not so—I did not read that book—I don't know anything about it—I never saw "——

" Stop !" Mr. Rogers exclaimed, justly shocked at what seemed to him the amazing hardihood of her falsehood. " I cannot listen to such protestations ; they make me shudder. Do not add any more sins to those you are already involved in."

" Let me ask one question," said Miss Barlow, eagerly. " Can you deny that that is the book you were reading before Chapel, on Tuesday morning ?"

" Miss Barlow, I do not wish this conversation prolonged "——

" Yes," cried Louie, " I do deny it—Mr. Rogers I did not read that book then, or any other time—I was reading "——

" What ?"

A strange faltering and hesitancy came into her manner, as she attempted an answer and failed in it.

" Go and get me the book you were reading then," he said ; and she started forward and hurried eagerly out of the room.

Several minutes elapsed without her return; so

many, indeed, that Mr. Rogers, to whose kind heart this scene was a severe trial, walked nervously up and down the room, and thought them interminably long; while Miss Barlow, who had a vague apprehension that Louie would attempt an escape, and might even now be flying down town, bonnetless and wild, to catch the train just due at the depot, suggested at last, had she not better go and look for her?

"No!" said Mr. Rogers, very simply and emphatically.

At length, however, the door opened; Mr. Rogers stood still, and Miss Barlow glanced up quickly as Louie entered. But the flushed and angry face was altered altogether now, they saw, as they regarded it inquiringly. A look of stolid determination had settled on it, a white cold look of hopelessness and wretchedness. She stood still for a moment, after she had shut the door, then as if it cost her a great effort, she raised her eyes and said, in a husky, hurried voice:

"I know perfectly well what you will think—I cannot help it—the book is gone—I cannot find it."

"Ah!" escaped Miss Barlow's lips, so low, and yet *so* hateful.

"Very well; if you know what I think, you will not need the judgment of your conduct that it would pain me extremely to give you. I have done with you for the present. Take your books and go into one of the recitation rooms. Miss Emily's is unoccupied for the rest of the day, you may go there, and stay by yourself, with the exception of meal-time and study hour. You may prepare yourself to meet the Bishop this evening. That is all. You may go."

The heavy hours of solitude that succeeded, seemed ages of misery to Louie. When she first shut herself into the room she had been condemned to, she had been almost beside herself with passion, she had walked the floor and clenched her hands, till a violent burst of crying had relieved and subdued her; then tired out with her emotions, she had sunk into a sort of dull despair, nothing like repentance in her heart, only a rankling sense of injustice and a bitter resentment. Her head ached madly; if she only had some cold water to bathe her forehead with, a bandage to tie round her bursting temples; but to face all those girls in going upstairs for either, was worse than the worst headache that ever ached; and turning her back to the cruel sunlight that streamed in at the window, she laid her head on her folded arms, and never moved till startled by the great bell for dinner.

At the sound, she started up, and walking impatiently and agitatedly up and down the room, thought, " It will kill me to face them all. I cannot —will not go."

But then reason told her, it would be far more noticeable if she did not go: she would be sent for —brought down after all the rest were seated— any way, every one would soon know about it—they would soon know she was to be expelled— this time to-morrow, perhaps, it would be publicly given out before them all, she might as well get used to it. She would go down—she hated them all—hated them—what difference did it make to her what they thought? Did her face look so horribly, she wondered, would they guess how she felt? No, they shouldn't—she would be as unconcerned as any one—she *was* as unconcerned as any one, she repeated to herself, smoothing down her hair and hurrying up the stairs, and through the now empty halls.

But ah! poor child, or poor man, or poor woman, who has learned to dread meeting any eyes, cold or kind, of friend or foe, who shrinks with shame and pain from even a careless glance, who knows *by heart* the terrible lesson of disgrace. Perhaps there are harder things to bear, but this is very cruel. Sins that are only against Heaven and in *Its* sight, can be repented of and atoned for without that indescriba ble humiliation, that bitter sickening shame that is added when our fellows have been witnesses. God is so much gentler than men, "we feel it when we sorrow most," when we are lowest in His sight and in our own, and when we have done most to provoke Him to deny us: we would rather fall into His hands who can destroy both soul and body in hell, than into the hands of men as weak as we and only less contemptible.

No one can wonder at the double misery of the hour Louie spent under the eye of her schoolmates, nor at the eagerness with which she hurried out of their sight into solitude again, and began the long afternoon of that long day. It seemed a lifetime since morning. Tom and Col. Ruthven and her god-mother seemed to have been separated from her by months instead of hours. Everything was so strange and out of joint—so dreamy, and yet so staring and unalterable; there was but one tangible reality, her wretched, aching head—such pain as she never felt before, one moment a hot flash that seemed to go through every vein, and the next, a sick, faint feeling that made her lean down her head on the desk and wonder whether she would ever raise it up again. She tried not to think of what she had done, nor of what was coming; the hateful minutes that were so slow in going were yet too fast when she

thought of what this evening had in store for her.
The half of what she had said to Miss Barlow was
enough to make her dismissal from the school inevit-
able, she was sure.   What *had* she said to her?
She could not recall it distinctly—the very indis-
tinctness of the recollection made it alarming—perhaps she had been even more unpardonable than
she remembered—they had looked, indeed, struck
dumb with astonishment.   Even Miss Barlow had
never expected anything so bad of her.

Expelled from the school!   It is not easy to convey the shame and terror that the words inspired
her with.   Never in her time had such a thing happened to any one, but about two years before, a
girl had been expelled for some grave fault; and
the legend of her disgrace was whispered over to
this day—told to every new-comer, and kept fresh
in the minds of all.   The mantle of contempt had
fallen on her little sister, a pale, shy child, who had
remained after her.   She was avoided by her companions instinctively, had no chum whatever, and
lived in a strange sort of isolation among them all.
If she had been a merry, careless child, no doubt,
she would have made her way in the school, and
have cleared herself of the disgrace that now hung
around her; but she was sensitive and reserved, and
morbidly alive to the shame of her sister's punish-

6*

ment, that had happened when she was too young
to estimate it rightly, and that was unjustly punish-
ing her far more severely than it had ever done the
other; yet doing her more good, perhaps; for
though little Frances Chenilworth was growing up
under its shadow a timid, humble, lonely child, the
very shadow, no doubt, was keeping down the
faults for which her sister suffered, and which
might have marred her character as well, if the sunshine of praise and prosperity had fostered them.

Louie, proud and sensitive herself, had often
looked with wonder and pity at the neglected little
girl, not, of course, thinking of noticing or associat-
ing with her, for she gave no one a chance to think
of that; but Louie pondered: "If I were in her
place, I know I couldn't stand it. I couldn't live
without being liked or noticed by somebody. It
would just kill me to be so neglected and despised."

But it did not kill Frances; she went on in her
quiet, sad way, too inoffensive to be more than
neglected, too humble to be disliked, doing her
duty very simply, saying her prayers very faithfully, and living perhaps more entirely in the fear
and favor of God than any girl in the great school,
little as they guessed it.

Louie did not see or think of her very often—or,
rather, if she saw her often, she thought of her very

seldom; her colorless, quiet face and slight figure forever stooping over her books, were the sort of things that do not make much mark upon one's mind; they were too unobtrusive and too habitual to be striking. But somehow, to-day, since Louie had been alone down in Miss Emily's room, she had thought a great many times of Frances; more than of any other of her schoolmates. Perhaps she had begun to feel what that burden might be that she had borne so long, and possibly she wondered more that she could have been so patient. At any rate, the thought of her gave her a shadow of comfort; there was one among her companions whose sympathy she had a right to—who would not scorn her—and yet it was bitter to feel she had come to that! Come to be glad of the kindness of the most insignificant girl in school—almost glad of her pity.

Louie groaned aloud as she hid her face on the desk. Oh! if she could only hide it forever from every one's sight! It was a shame to meet any eyes now, even her mother's; that was perhaps the worst thought of all. She hated and despised herself so—she felt such a tempest of rage and resentment in her heart—she knew herself to be so disgraced and marked—that she dared not think of her mother's sweet, sad eyes, and put the thought out of her mind whenever it recurred to her.

She did not hear the door open, sitting stone still
with her head bowed down on her arms on the
desk; and Frances Chenilworth, entering noise-
lessly, did not see her till she was half-way into the
room. When she did perceive her, she gave a start
and turned back; but as she reached the door, she
glanced toward her again, and something in her attitude struck her with surprise and pity. She withdrew her hand from the knob of the door and timidly
took a step back into the room. Her face expressed
a great many shifting feelings, wonder at the
unusual sight of Louie crying, pity for her, fear of
rebuff, longing to give comfort, habitual shyness
and reserve struggling with an affectionate and
tender impulse. It was several minutes before,
standing beside her, she found courage to lay her
hand lightly on her arm, and whisper:

"Is there anything the matter with you?"

Louie gave a violent start and raised her head;
but, somehow, it did not seem to surprise her
exactly to see that it was Frances standing by her;
it was only the continuation of her long revery; she
only shook her head, and half-turned it away without saying anything. But Frances had not ceased
to be sorry for her since she had seen her face, and
not taking her silence for a rebuff, she went on
timidly after a minute:

"I hope nobody has been unkind to you; but you mustn't mind if they have. Perhaps they didn't mean it; very often people don't, when it seems very hard; they only don't think how it would feel themselves—they never put themselves in anybody else's place."

"Ah!" thought Louie, "how well you know all that!" But aloud she said: "Yes! everybody has been unkind to me—everybody—and I don't care *that*, Frances. I don't care for anybody."

Frances looked troubled.

"I'm glad if you don't care in the right sort of a way, but"——

"Oh, I don't care in the way people don't care when they pull the trigger of a pistol within two inches of their brains—that's the way I don't care. I'm not your way; I'm not meek; I don't want you to suppose I am. You'd be afraid of me if you knew how I felt; I'm sometimes half afraid of myself."

"I wish you wouldn't talk so," said Frances, uneasily. "I know you're not in earnest, but it sounds dreadfully. You won't like to remember it in Chapel this evening."

"I don't know that I shall be allowed to go into Chapel. I am sentenced to be kept by myself, Frances. I am too bad to go near the girls. Mr.

explain what it was she saw and lived under and looked at hourly and depended upon for the pleasure of her life.

"What do you mean—why wouldn't you dare to stay away? Suppose you were not fit?"

"Nobody is fit really."

"Not perfect, Frances, but better than other people, different from other people. I don't understand how any girl can go till she is really good, and knows she can keep so."

"Nobody can know that; and if a person waited when once she had been told, that would be a sin in itself, a dreadful sin."

"How can it be a sin, if you know you are not fit?"

"It must be a sin," said Frances, speaking quickly, "to live in neglect of any command that God has taken the trouble to give us, and to disobey His last request; to say we are not ready to receive Him when He is ready to come; to acknowledge by doing it that we have no life in us and are not concerned that we have not; to refuse to do the one thing He asked of us that last night before the awful Friday. Oh, Louie! don't you see how dreadful it is? Don't it make you tremble to see the people go out of church?"

"It's all dreadful," she said, with a shudder.

"It's dreadful to disobey—but it's ten times worse to be unworthy and to live as some people do, just as bad as they were before, not a bit as if they were Christians, not a bit as if there were any difference between them and the world."

"We must not think about that, we don't know their hearts."

"But, Frances," said Louie, abruptly, as she paused, "I wish you'd tell me—don't that chapter in Corinthians frighten you? It keeps running in my head all the time, and when I see the others going to the altar, I can't think of anything else—I can't help thinking how they dare. That awful, awful verse! It haunts me so!"

"Do you mean—'He that eateth and drinketh unworthily?'"

"Yes."

"It always frightened me, too, till that sermon Mr. Rogers preached in Chapel, one stormy Sunday, when we couldn't go to church—it was two months ago. Don't you remember it?"

"It must have been before I came back. I don't recollect anything about it. What did he say?"

"He said—I can't remember exactly what he said—only it made it very different. I believe he said that it was a letter written to the Corinthians, who were in such different circumstances from us,

that we could not take it all to ourselves. They
had been growing very loose and irreverent in their
celebration of the Lord's Supper, preceding it by
their 'Agapæ,' or feasts of charity, at which the rich
were careless and intemperate, and the poor were
neglected. And so St. Paul wrote to warn them of
their danger and set them right about it's being a
spiritual feast, and one that should be celebrated
with reverence and great solemnity, and in no way
profaned or partaken of thoughtlessly. And it is
in this sense, he said, we were to take it; and that
word, too, that sounds so awful, 'damnation,'
meant only 'judgment' or 'condemnation,' and
was often translated so in other parts of the Bible,
indeed, in another part of this very chapter. So
you can very well see how the Corinthians might
indeed bring a judgment upon themselves by the
way they had got in of slighting the Holy Communion, and treating it as any other feast; and I'm
sure it's a comfort to know it is not all meant for
us. Though, oh, there's enough required of us to
make us fearful; but how can we expect to get
help if we disobey? He has told us to do it, and we
must do it, or be living in open rebellion against
Him. He said—you know what it was—' he that
cometh to Me '—and if we come, no matter how
miserable and young and ignorant, and even

wicked, we are, we shall not—cannot be cast out—
but helped and comforted and made better, led
from 'strength to strength,' slowly perhaps,
and sadly, but surely, for there can be no doubt
about His promise. If we only believe and try—
if we only say, 'I do believe it is the only thing
that will help me, I will do as God has told me to
do, though I don't see the way to make myself fit—
I will just mind Him and do the best I can, and
hope and trust He will accept my good and sincere
wish to do as I believe He wishes.' That is all He
requires of us for a beginning—Oh, dear Louie, if
I could only tell you—if I could only make you
understand what a sure help it is; how much better
than anything else in the world. It may not come
right away, it may be ever so long before the
doubts and fears go away, but you know there *can't*
be any uncertainty about the promise; in time, it
must come good to you—only, only try."

"Oh!" murmured Louie, "you don't know half
how bad I am, how angry, and envious and unfor-
giving—you wouldn't tell me to think about Communion, if you knew my heart."

"It will never be any better till you do. God
won't hear your prayer till you consent to do that
one thing He requires of you. No matter how hard
you plead, if you don't consent to *obey*, He won't

have anything to do with you. Don't fancy you can get at holiness your own way—you can't. You must take His way, whether it seems wise to you or not; you must just mind Him, and then He will not fail to help and govern you, and bring you up in His steadfast fear and love. And forgive you, oh! with all His heart, and be *so* merciful! How can you—how can anybody refuse such kindness, and choose such awful, awful sin and danger?"

"Don't say such things, you frighten me," murmured Louie.

"I don't frighten you any more than you frighten me," said the girl, in a smothered voice, her grey eyes dilating and darkening as she spoke, and her white fingers clasping each other tightly over the book she held. "It frightens me—it almost kills me, when I think of all the girls going on in such sin; when I think of their danger, I am almost sick with fear. I cannot tell you —I never told anybody—I never talked to anybody before—I can't ask them, I can't say a word to them; but it makes me so wretched! Long hours at night, when they are all asleep so quietly, it seems to me sometimes I shall go wild with thinking of their souls—their souls that they are throwing away. No life in them—do you know that? Careless and quiet and easy, and yet before the night is over they may be required of them. Oh, God knows I pray !—God knows I would give anything to turn them "——

"Don't—don't talk so!" cried Louie, raising her head. "It makes me miserable. You have always been good—you don't know how it feels to be full of wicked, stubborn thoughts—to feel as if you hated people, as if there was nothing but wickedness in you—to feel as if you had no right to think of going "——

"I do know, I know better than you do. You have friends and have something to keep you from uncharitableness, but everybody turns away from me, and I have had to forgive them all. I used to think I never could. I used to think, before I was confirmed, I never could get used to it; but I have, I don't think anything about it now, I am perfectly certain it's all right."

"Frances, you must forgive my part; I never knew anything about it; I never thought "——

"There is nothing to forgive," said Frances, leaning back, with a low sigh, the strange look passing out of her eyes, as she regained her usual manner; "I have no claim on anybody; I am very useless and don't do any one any good; I ought not to expect any love."

"If my love is worth anything, you will always

have mine.   Oh, Frances, won't you be my friend!
I need you more than you need me."

"I never had a friend; I don't know how to be
of any good to any one," said the girl, with a
momentary cloud of pain passing over her sensitive
face.

"Oh, help me!" cried Louie, catching her hand.
"Tell me how you ever grew to be so good. I am so
wretched; I can't tell you half how desperate. It's
all tangled and miserable. I am almost tired of
longing to be better—I am so tired, I sometimes
wish I could die. Yes, die; don't look so troubled.
It is wicked, but it's no wickeder than half my
other thoughts; I don't think I am afraid to die,
not half as much afraid as I am to go on living this
wretched life, doing wrong all the time, and with
a gnawing pain at my heart forever."

"Don't you see, then, that God wants you to be
better—that He cannot give you up, though you go
on disobeying and denying Him! That pain will
grow worse and worse if you won't listen to it till
it kills your soul "——

"Hush! you must not say such things," cried
Louie, hiding her face and shuddering. "Don't be
so cruel; only tell me what to do—only teach me
how to be better—fit to live, if I am not fit to die.
I don't care whether I live or die, if I can *only* get

forgiven. Sit down by me again; don't go away. If you won't say such dreadful things, I will do anything you tell me to. Read to me in your book—talk to me quietly. Oh! if you knew how my head ached!"

It was twilight in Miss Emily's room before Frances went away. Louie shuddered a little as she let her go, but she was now quieted and comforted enough to bear the gloom of the half hour that preceded tea-time. She sat down in the window, trying to keep sight of what daylight was left as long as she could, and then essayed repeating from memory all the "Words for the Day" and hymns she could recollect. But they were evanescent and hard to arrest; she felt too weak and too sick to remember anything correctly or make any mental effort; she could only say them over to herself till she grew dreamy and listless; her half-closed eyes rested on the fast-fading light in the western sky, and her thoughts wandered far away across cold leagues of ocean, to the sweet Italian home, where her mother perhaps and Larry were welcoming her father as he came back from his long day on board ship. That soft, rosy sky—not cold and grey like this—was shining on the face she loved so much. Was it mournful to-night, she wondered? Had mother a thought for her? Did

7

her hand touch vacantly and listlessly Larry's pretty curls, as he played around her knee, and her kind smile die faintly when he looked away? And for the others, was the smile as short-lived and were the eyes as absent?

"Ah! mother, mother, if you only knew!"

Yes, if she only knew; but One tenderer even than she knows—knows and pities.

CHAPTER IX.

THE BISHOP.

"They best can bind who have been bruisèd oft."

"I WILL leave you; you may wait here till the Bishop comes."

Mr. Rogers said this as he left the Study, preceded by Miss Barlow. Louie bent her head mechanically; the words did not convey much to her. She sat down by the table when they left her alone, and, with a dull, tired feeling, leaned her head on her hand and watched the flicker of the gaslight, and traced out the pattern on the paper shade over it.

The Bishop was coming, then. Well, that was very frightful, but, somehow, she was too tired to be frightened. She only longed for it to be over, that she might go upstairs and go to bed. The Bishop knew all about it; she would not have the trouble of trying to tell him. He knew she had been openly and outrageously disrespectful to Miss Barlow—had insulted her, in fact—and that, be-

sides that, and the complaints of Miss Marbais and
Mr. Van Buren, she was convicted of so much
deceit and such a falsehood about the novel, that
she must be prepared for his severest displeasure.
It seemed, indeed, as plain as daylight, that Louie
was persisting in a falsehood. Nothing but her
word against all this evidence. At first, the accusation had roused her to extremest anger, but she
soon grew aware of the apparent justice of its injustice, and the hopelessness of her case; and, cal-
lous and sullen, she had sunk into an indifference
from which, in the half-hour's interview she had
just passed through, Mr. Rogers had failed to rouse
her. He was disheartened and uneasy; nothing
since he had charge of the school had vexed him
more. Here was a girl upon whom kindness
seemed to make no impression, and whom severity
only seemed to harden. He could have dealt with
her obstinacy and willfulness, if that had been all,
but this discovery of habitual deceitfulness, and this
open and shameless persistence in a falsehood,
while it steeled his heart completely against her,
threw him into great doubt as to the course he
ought to pursue. Such an example as this might
do endless mischief in the school—had, he feared,
already done it; prompt measures must be taken to
reduce her to submission, or show the others that

such insubordination could not be tolerated. While
he had a strong concern for the good of the one,
the many must not be sacrificed to it.

Mr. Rogers, though a very kind, and just, and
sensible man, was a fallible man for all that, and
could not see, through the obscuring mists of error
and misfortune and mistake that hung around
Louie, into the real honesty and misery of her
heart. Not one person in twenty could have seen
it; not one in twenty but would have treated her
with double the harshness that he did. Indeed, it
is hardly fair to call it harshness; he was too much
grieved to be harsh, but his manner was so plain
an indication of his feelings that it sent a chill of
hopelessness to her heart. How could she ever
make him believe her—was there any use in trying? Would any one believe her? No! She
would not try—she would not say another word.
They might do anything they pleased with her, she
did not care, she would not answer nor defend herself. They meant to frighten her into submission
by sending her to the Bishop—the Bishop would be
here in five minutes, and—she did not care. He
was very much displeased, Mr. Rogers had made
her understand. She had sometimes fancied, when
she had watched his face in church in the pauses of
the service, that it would be a very terrible thing to

see it hardened into displeasure—the very worst thing, indeed, that could happen; but now she said to herself, actually, she did not care.

And she was not very far mistaken about her feelings, perhaps. The thread of injustice that ran through the complaints against her, just gave her enough to hold by to resent all the rest. She was very bad, she knew that. She was rebellious and self-willed, and had long been heedless and inattentive; she was bitterly sorry for all this, and had meant to mend, till they threw upon her this shameful imputation of dishonesty. An accusation that roused her as no other could have done, for never having been cowardly or mean in disposition, she had never been tempted to prevarication or deceit, but spoke the truth and acted "out and out" as she felt, as many a timider but better child has lacked the strength to do. She scorned deceit; in fact, it had never been her temptation, and she did not fairly know what it meant. She knew what hatred, and malice, and uncharitableness meant; she knew what pride, and self-will, and disobedience meant; but, except to loathe and despise them in others, she did not know what falsehood and intriguing meant.

And so, when such a suspicion was cast upon her, at first it made her passionately angry; but when she felt it fastening itself upon her, and had to own

there was no help, and saw with her own eyes, there
was a look of truth about the bitter, shameful lie,
she ceased to struggle as it tightened around her,
and worn out and reckless, sunk down beneath it.

Several minutes passed before she heard the hall
door open. How well she knew that step across the
hall! she had listened to its quick echoes too often
down the long passage that led to the chapel not to
know what presence it intimated.

Was she frightened? There was a sort of choking in her throat for a minute as she heard Mr.
Rogers' voice outside in a low parley, but before the
Study door opened, she was stolid, stubborn and indifferent again. She rose mechanically as it closed
upon the new-comer, lifting her eyes for one glance,
then fastening them upon the floor again. Yes,
that was the face she had imagined in church, that
was the very, very look she feared, only so much
worse, as much worse as facts are than fancies when
we come to face them.

It suited well the slow, deliberate voice that met
her ear, that strange sympathetic moving voice, that
stern as it was, swept away all the pride and stubbornness in her heart. He believed she was guilty;
he was telling her so, and of the pain it gave him to
believe such a thing of one of the children whom
he prayed with and for daily, whose souls were in

his care; he asked her earnestly and as if his heart
were in the question, if, since he must believe it, he
might not also find she had resolved to acknowledge
and repent of it?

A nightmare seemed choking the words that
rushed to her lips, she tried to speak, but no sound
came; she tried to raise her eyes, but they sunk before they met the eyes fastened so scrutinizingly
upon her. Oh, if she could only speak, if she
could only tell him! She felt as if she should die if
he went on believing her guilty; it was little to her
now what any one else thought, but she must make
him understand. There! The pause had passed, he
had begun to speak again, and he was thinking her
obstinate and unmoved, and his tone, though it was
not harder and colder, as she feared, had such a solemnity in it that she hardly heard the words, hardly
dared to think what they might mean.

The precious minutes were slipping away, the
only chance she might ever have to tell him—it was
cruel that she could not speak; and when he paused
again, the effort to command her voice, the terror
lest she should not make him understand, made such
bewildering confusion in her aching head, that a
giddiness came over her, and she could only grasp
the chair before her for support, and shut her eyes
from the glare of the gaslight on the table.

"My child," he said, with a sudden change of voice, "have we misunderstood you after all? Only tell me what you have done, I will promise to believe you."

At that instant, the Chapel bell began to ring for evening service, and that sound, with its double reminder of her sin and its consequence, broke down all the desperation and fear that had combined to make up her outward calmness. She sank down in the chair on which she had been leaning, and bowing her head on the table, burst into a passion of tears. She had forgotten all but that she was forbidden to go to Chapel, that Mr. Rogers had said she was to go away by herself and neither take her meals nor go to prayers nor join in any way with her companions. Chapel had often been irksome to her before; she had often heard the bell with regret for her interrupted amusement or work, and had wondered that it came so soon and recurred so often; but now, since all this trouble had come upon her, and since Frances had shown her where it had begun, she felt the wildest longing to kneel again among the children, and hear the absolution she had so often neglected to appropriate, and pray for the peace it promised. It seemed to her, that to hear that bell stop, and the doors close upon the Bishop and the assembled children, and know that she was shut out, would be worse than any terror she had ever known, too hopeless and cruel for belief.

"Oh, sir!" she cried, lifting her head and speaking in a broken, hurried voice, "let me go to Chapel. I know you don't believe me, I know nobody does; I know you think I am not fit to go among the others; but it will kill me if I am shut out—you don't know how it frightens me. Let me go to-night—let me go this once."

"Tell me first," he said, looking thoughtfully at her, "why you want to go. Is it because you do not wish the girls to see you are disgraced, or have you a better reason?"

"I don't care about the girls, they'll all know it soon enough, if they don't know it now. It isn't that—it's only for myself I want to go, I am so frightened, so ·miserable. Oh, sir! if I could only tell you, if you would only believe me!"

"My poor child, I do, I will believe you."

She stretched out her hands with an eager gesture and hurried on: "I have been so bad, wrong about everything, self-willed and proud and hateful, I never dreamed one could get in one short summer so far wrong. Oh! I never could tell you half my impatience and wickedness—getting worse and worse all the time. I see it all now, I know what it is all for; I know I deserve that every one should think ill of me, it is no wonder I am so punished. I want to tell you—only it is of no use—I don't expect you to believe me—but I never read that book. I never saw it before. I haven't read a novel since I came here. I don't know how it came by me on the bed. I did not know a thing about it till Mr. Rogers showed it to me. Oh sir! please believe me—please believe I would not lie. How could I!"

"Aye, how could you!" he repeated in a low tone, as if to himself, as he looked thoughtfully at her.

"I know it all looks black enough. I don't blame them for thinking as they do, it would be strange if they did not. Everything is against me, even mother's book is gone. I cannot find that to show them, I could not even bear to tell them what it was. It seemed to me, when I found it was gone out of my desk, as if she had deserted me too. I have hunted everywhere—everywhere—but there is no use, it is gone."

" You left it in your desk you say—this book ?"

" Yes, I always kept it there. At first I had it upstairs on the shelf with my Bible, but one of the girls laughed, and I was ashamed and took it downstairs and kept it under my other books. I'd give anything I've got to see it once again, even though it didn't clear me, for it was mother's last souvenir, just as I left her on the ship that day, and she whispered to me; read it every day; and I promised her I would, and oh, it makes me sick to think how miserably I have neglected it! Sometimes I have forgotten it for days together, and I shouldn't have remembered it that morning, only there had been something on Sunday about keeping promises that made me think of it, and I resolved to come down early every morning and read before Chapel. It was very careless in me not to listen for the stopping of the bell; I don't how it happened, and then Miss Barlow was very angry, and I was very disrespectful, and so it has gone on. And now they all believe I have told a falsehood, and am persisting in it, and nothing I can say will change them."

"Did you tell Mr. Rogers this?"

"I don't know exactly what I told him, I can't remember half that happened, my head has ached so awfully. I didn't—no—I am sure now I didn't tell him about the 'Sacra Privata;' Miss Barlow was by, and I couldn't."

"What difference did that make?"

"I can't explain exactly, sir. I don't know how it is, only she makes me so wicked—even if she doesn't say a word, I'm just as angry as I can be the minute I come near her. I thought I had forgiven her, and was all done with such sort of feelings this afternoon after I had been talking to Frances, but the first minute she came into the room to-night, they were all back. But I do forgive her, I do really. I am not angry, I shall feel so different if you will let me go to Chapel. I am sure I shall feel better after Chapel—Oh, sir! Think how I need it. And after all, it can't hurt any one, my going. I am no worse than I have been this long time—Mr. Rogers couldn't be angry if you let me."

"Child, how can you think there is any need of such pleading?"

"You will not refuse me?" she interrupted, in an agony of earnestness, as the last vibration of the Chapel bell swung upon the air.

"My child," and a gentle hand touched the bowed head, "prayers and pardon and peace are for such as you. Only such as feel the guilt and burden of their sins can fully meet the Presence that waits within holy walls; for them He is ' waiting to be gracious,' for their prayers alone His ear is open. You were never fitter to seek Him than you are to-night, He never loved you better than He does to-night, His boundless love and pity are stooping down from Heaven to infold you, His gracious heart is yearning to forgive you. Only go to

Him, my child. Go to Him with your sins upon your head, and ask Him to take them away. Tell Him all that is in your heart, tell Him all your hope is in Him, that there is nothing else but His forgiveness that can do you any good. He will not doubt you, He will not misapprehend you. He is as infinitely true and just as He is kind. His favor is better than life itself. Once make that yours and you will not mind the rest. You will not mind coldness and suspicion and misconstruction. It will hardly pain you that no one else knows your heart if He does. A love that passeth knowledge, a peace that the world can neither give nor take away, a hope that is strong as no human hope can be—such are the rewards He has for them that seek Him, even here. So He makes up to them their share of happiness, even here. My child, it is a blessed service, it is a blessed peace. Ask Him for it on your knees to-night, and He cannot, will not send you empty away. He has never failed them that seek Him yet, He will not begin with the last, the weakest, the youngest of His flock."

It must have been the dawning of the promised peace that stilled the storm so entirely while she listened to these words; she did not lift her head nor speak when he paused; there was such a stillness in the room, in all the house, in her heart. All were in the Chapel waiting for the Bishop; there was not a footfall nor a sound throughout the deserted halls and empty rooms; and after a moment, through the half-closed doors,

> " A rolling organ-harmony
> Swells up and shakes and falls."

Louie started a little and raised her head, recalled to the almost forgotten present. The Bishop had put on his surplice, and said, stretching out his hand to her.

"Come, my child, they are waiting."

It was so strange, so dreamy, following him through the hall toward the Chapel, from which the distant music was swelling, their steps echoing audibly through the emptiness; the lights, faint and dim. At the Chapel door he paused and laid his hand for a moment on her head.

"May God bless this service to your soul."

Then opening the door, he preceded her into the Chapel.

CHAPTER X.

" All without is mean and small,
  All within is vast and tall ;
  All without is harsh and shrill,
  All within is hushed and still.

" Jesus, let me enter in,
  Wrap me safe from noise and sin.
  Jesus, Lord, my heart will break,
  Save me for Thy great love's sake."

KINGSLEY.

MISS BARLOW'S girls sat in the last row of seats but
one at the other end of the Chapel, so there was a
long trial to Louie before she gained her seat—or
rather, would have been, if she had had a thought
of any of the things that are seen ; if the things of
eternity, the presence of God, the peril of her soul,
had not been the real, the actual to her then. At
any time in her life before, it would have been a
trial to her to have known that as she came into
the lighted Chapel, there were so many keen young
eyes turned upon her, so many looks of wonder
following her to her seat. There had been a sort

160

of lull in the music, it was soft and low as they entered; they had been waiting some minutes for the Bishop's entrance, and every eye was fastened on the door as his well-known step was heard approaching, and when there entered with him this unexpected attendant, there was involuntary surprise on every face, and as she turned down the aisle toward her place, and the Bishop turned the other way and went toward the chancel, the fickle, wondering little faces bent curiously forward and gazed after the one that most excited their curiosity.

But Louie did not heed; the row upon row of attentive faces, the stillness, the soft, bright lights, might have been the adjuncts of a misty dream, they were not realities to her. She heeded the living multitude around her no more than we heed the witnesses, who, we are told, "hold us in full survey," the saints, whose faith is changed to sight, the angels, who always behold the face of our Father in Heaven. There was but one thought. She was in the presence of God—but one desire, to be forgiven of Him, to be received of Him.

And that service *was* blessed to her soul. It was a service unmixed with one thought of the miserable world that mixes too much with all our best services, untainted with one wish, one longing that

was separate from His will whom she worshipped.
God help us! who go so loiteringly and pray so
listlessly! The way might not be so long, the
prayers required so weary, and so many times
repeated, if they were more real, more vivid, more
entire.   One.service, such as this, might save us
years of sacrifice; might bring us nearer to that
Holiness, without which we cannot see our Lord,
than half a lifetime spent in such worship as we
have grown to think is the best our nature is capable of.

"Hear my prayer, O Lord, and consider my
desire; hearken unto me for Thy truth and righte-
ousness' sake.

"And enter not into judgment with thy servant;
for in Thy sight shall no man living be justified."

Louie, on her knees, her face hidden in her hands,
had tried to find words for her wants, had tried to
utter the thoughts her heart was bursting with; but
it was all a tumult of passionate repentance, an
utter self-abasement, a prostrate cry for mercy,
wordless and voiceless, audible only to Him who
knows our necessities before we ask.   She had
heard the others rise to their feet a moment after
she had entered; she was still kneeling, and she
pressed her hands before her face, as the many
voices, low and full, chanted this prayer, the very

prayer she had been wanting to find the words for, the prayer of which her heart had been so full. It seemed to her almost as if the angels had seen into her soul, and pitying her ignorance and confusion and misery, had bent themselves before the Great White Throne, and breathed for her the prayer she heard—so low, far off, unearthly it sounded to her ears.

But it took half the burden off her heart; the actual putting into words of her dreadful self-reproach seemed to take away its pain; and when the music ceased, she rose from her knees, quieted and almost peaceful.

There was a moment's stillness, and then the voice that had always brought her comfort, read:

"The sacrifices of God are a broken spirit; a broken and a contrite heart, O God, Thou wilt not despise."

There was no danger that He would despise this one now offered to Him. The last, the youngest, the weakest, to such He is ever tenderest, of such He has made His Kingdom to consist.

CHAPTER XI.

CORRUPTION AND BRIBERY.

"O what a tangled web we weave
When first we practise to deceive!"

SCOTT.

"STUPID! stop when I call you, why don't you?" Addy McFarlane said, with more energy than she ordinarily used, laying a correspondingly emphatic grasp upon Alice Aulay's shoulder, who was trying to hurry past her into the playground.

"How can I stop?" Alice replied, fretfully, trying to free herself with as much impatience as she dared to show. "I'm in a great hurry. Julia is waiting for me."

"What does Julia want of you, pray?"

"Why I've something to tell her, she sent me to find out something for her—let go, Addy—let go, please do."

"Oh ho!" said Addy, letting go of the white shoulder on which her hand had left a mark, but keeping, as a hostage, an end of a long, light curl

164

between her fingers, while she changed her tone of authority to one of coaxing kindness. "I say, Ally, do you want me to look out those capitals for you? I'd just as soon—I haven't anything else to do before school. Bring your map, and sit down here by me on the steps."

"No, thank you," said Alice, with some dignity, withdrawing to the extremest limits of the long curl, which Adelaide firmly retained. "Julia's found all but three for me, and those I promised her I'd do for myself. She's got my map out under the apple-tree with her, and she's waiting. I *wish* you'd let me go!"

"Oh you little gipsy! I don't see why you're always after Julia; I never can get you to stay near me. What does Julia do to make you so mighty fond of her?"

"Why, she doesn't do anything," returned Alice, feeling very important. "She's so beautiful and so good, nobody can help being fond of her."

"That's true," said Adelaide, meditatively; "she's the prettiest girl in *our* dormitory, by all odds."

"In any dormitory," cried Alice, with enthusiasm.

"Well, yes, perhaps so. Georgy Reynolds is pretty, but then she's so conceited, and Susie McAllister's face gets in such a blaze whenever

she's spoken to, that it spoils all *her* good looks.
Now, Julia's so quiet and sweet, and has such nice
manners, that nobody can help liking her."

"She's so good! I'd give anything to be like
her."

"Yes, she's a very good girl, and I shouldn't
wonder if you were as good when you're as old.
I don't believe you'll look like her, though; you'll
be prettier."

"*What!*"

"Why, you'll be prettier than Julia, when you're
her age," said Adelaide, with a quiet eye on her
little companion's face. "You'll be taller, you
know; Julia's too short. And her hair don't curl;
yours will be down to your knees in ringlets by
the time you're grown up."

"How foolish you are!" said Alice, feeling very
hot and twisting her head away, but quite disposed
to hear a little more. "I don't think light hair is
pretty a bit; I like brown hair, such as Julia's, a
great deal better."

"Ah, no!" and Adelaide shook her head.
"There's nothing so sweet as light curls. I wish
my hair would curl."

"Don't it at all?" asked Alice, curiously, looking with much interest at Adelaide's flaxen braids,
and realizing more fully than she had ever done be-

fore the unspeakable value of the adornments of her head. "I should think it might, if you tried it."

"Not the least use. I've wet it, and twisted it, and put it up in papers, but it don't do it a bit of good. It's just as straight as a candle—there's no curl to it."

"All our family have curly hair," Alice said, involuntarily straightening herself up, and giving a complacent toss to the admired ringlets. "Why, little Sister Lilly's hair isn't so long as mine, but it curls all over her head. Papa says it shall be cut off, it takes nurse so long to fix it every day."

"Oh, it would be a shame to cut it off!" said Adelaide, warmly. "I am sure your papa wouldn't be so unkind."

She had secured Alice for the present, she saw, and concluded she might drop the curl, figuratively and literally, without danger of losing its owner; so, letting the ringlet slip from her fingers, she leaned back with a yawn, and said, listlessly:

"I wonder what makes me so tired! Would you mind, Ally, running into the schoolroom and looking in my desk for a package of dough-balls—it's lying on the top of my Analyse."

'I'll go, certainly," Alice replied, obeying with alacrity.

When the little fly came back, she did not need

a second invitation to sit down on the steps beside
Adelaide and share the contents of the package.
"Dough-balls" were her acknowledged passion;
her weekly sixpence never knew any other appropriation; and the only regret she ever felt in thus
investing it, was the little way it went toward
satisfying her appetite for the purchased delicacy.
Sixpence was considered, among the Primaries, as
quite a handsome income—even the girls in Middle
D. looked upon it as a comfortable little thing to
be sure of; but, ah, the insufficiency of it to meet
this young spendthrift's cravings!

" Why, Julia, if there was any way of making it
go further," she had said to Julia one day, and
Julia had laughed and hurt her feelings very
deeply. But after a while, Julia had been induced
to give the subject greater attention, and had come
to the conclusion, with Alice, that nothing more
profitable could be done about it, if dough-balls
were her fixed desire. Sixpence would buy just
six dough-balls, and no more. Alice had hoped that
if she became a regular subscriber for that amount,
something might be thrown in—half a dough-ball
a week, say; or seven every other week. But the
" candy woman " wouldn't hear to it; she didn't
make anything on the dough-balls anyhow, she
said; she only kept 'em for the accommodation of

the young ladies at the Hall. Nobody else ever thought of calling for 'em. So Alice had to give up all hope of such an arrangement, and make herself contented with stretching out the weekly six as far as they would go. And that was a very little way, indeed; her purchase was always made on Saturday afternoon, and the last dough-ball generally went under her pillow that night, crushed up in a sticky handful of brown paper, to be pulled out and eaten the first thing in the morning. Then followed a dreary blank, a whole week uncheered by confectionery. Alice counted the days till Saturday.

Consider, then, what her enthusiasm must have been when Adelaide invited her to " help herself" out of an untouched paper of dough-balls. She ate No. 1 without stopping for breath, then looked with great, greedy eyes at Adelaide, who was nibbling rather daintily at hers.

"Take another, child," she said; and Alice, with an overpowering sensation of gratitude, and the conviction that Addy McFarlane was the best-natured girl that ever lived, took another, and ate it a little more deliberately, but with infinite relish.

"We shan't more than finish these before the bell rings, shall we?" said Addy, looking at the paper. " But then, you said you were going to tell Julia a message, didn't you?"

"Oh, it wasn't a message," returned the little girl, hastily. "There's no particular hurry; it was only something she wanted me to find out about."

"Upon my word, how useful you are! Does Julia trust you to do errands for her?"

"Why, of course, she does. I've been about one ever since breakfast for her."

"Well, did you get through it?"

"Yes, as far as I can. But then I can't find out much till noon. Mrs. Seward is so busy, she couldn't tell me much."

"Why, what on earth did you have to ask of Mrs. Seward?"

"Oh, about Louie Atterbury, you know. Julia's so wretched about her, she don't know what to do. When she saw her bed was empty this morning when we got up, and that she didn't come to Chapel either, she was *so* frightened, I know she cried all during prayers, and she made me watch for Mrs. Seward till the breakfast bell rang, to ask her what the matter was, or where Louie had gone. She was afraid to ask Miss Barlow; Miss Barlow looked so thundering cross."

"Well, did you see Mrs. Seward before breakfast?"

"No; Mrs. Seward didn't come down till we were all at the table, and went up before we had

finished, and poor Julia couldn't eat a bit of breakfast. I didn't think she cared so much about Louie.
I don't care a great deal what the matter with her
is, except that Julia cares."

" Well, did you find out ?"

" Not exactly, but then a good deal. I've been
waiting outside the Nursery door ever since breakfast, for Mrs. Seward to come out, and though I
heard her voice, very low, and the doctor's inside
for ever so long, she didn't open the door till about
ten minutes ago. Then she came out to call a
servant. She had a glass and a spoon in her hand,
and she seemed to be in great hurry, for when I
spoke to her she didn't answer, and generally, you
know, she is so good to me ! So I waited till she'd
given her order, and then I pulled her dress a little,
and asked her if she'd please tell me if Louie Atterbury was sick."

" What did she say ?"

" Yes, very sick, I am afraid, my child," she said ;
and then she was going away, but I kept hold of
her dress, and begged her to tell me about it, for
Julia was so unhappy. And then she stopped, and
put her arm around me, and said she remembered
Julia and Louie were great friends, and that I must
tell Julia not to be uneasy, she hoped it would not
be very serious, but that Louie had been very ill in

the night. Miss Barlow had come to her room and waked her in a great fright, for Louie was in a high fever, and talked so wildly. Don't you wonder we all slept through it? But then it takes a good deal to wake girls, Mrs. Seward says."

"Well?"

'Then Mrs. Seward brought Louie into the nursery, and they watched by her all night, and as soon as it was daylight, they sent for the doctor. She's quieter now, but she's out of her head yet. I heard her talking after Mrs. Seward went in, and Mrs. Seward said 'poor child!' and tried to coax her to lie still and go to sleep. Mrs. Seward said I might come up again at the noon recess, and she'd tell me how she was by that time."

"That's all you've got to tell Julia, then?"

"No," said Alice, dropping her voice a little. "There's something else. I didn't come right down, I waited a minute outside the door. I thought I heard somebody talking, and that perhaps it was Louie—but it wasn't."

"Who?"

"I wasn't listening exactly—you know—I didn't mean to—that is "——

"Of course, I understand. It was all right. Go on."

"Miss Stanton was there, and she and Mrs. Seward were talking about Louie. They said ever so

much that I couldn't understand, then Miss Stanton
moved nearer to the door and I heard better.
There's been a great fuss, I should think from what
they said, and Louie has been doing something
dreadful. Mrs. Seward said, she couldn't have
believed it of her, and so did Miss Stanton. And
they said Mr. Rogers thought she ought to be
expelled, and Miss Barlow had said she should
resign her place if she was not, and Miss Stanton
did not really know what ought to be done. Miss
Barlow had been so very much tried with her, and
it ruined her authority with the others so entirely
to have such continual contests with her, that she
could not blame her exactly for the position she
had taken. She wished very much it had not
occurred. It placed them all so uncomfortably.
There was no turning Miss Barlow; she had said it,
and she would not retract, and Mr. Rogers was disposed to think she was not altogether unreasonable. But strangest of all—and here they talked
so low I couldn't catch much—but it was pretty
near like this—that the Bishop took Louie's part,
and would not say that he believed her guilty, that
all the evidence could not convince him, and that
he had said she should not be punished yet. And
altogether, it was likely to make a great row
among the teachers before it was all over."

"But tell me, Alice," said Adelaide, eagerly, "didn't you hear anything about what she'd done? Couldn't you get any idea of what it was?"

"It was something about a book—a novel—and then she'd told a story, a very bad one—about something, and been dreadfully bad to Miss Barlow."

"Ah!" and Adelaide's lips parted in a hateful smile of satisfaction. "They found she'd been reading novels, then? What did they say—how did they find out?"

"I don't know, I couldn't get that. Only I know as soon as Louie is well enough they're going to have it all up before the school, and the Bishop is going to examine all about it; and there is a girl, they didn't say who, that Miss Barlow says will be able to throw a great deal of light upon the subject."

"They didn't say what her name was?"

"No; Miss Barlow had said, though, that her testimony would settle it all, that she was a girl who stood very well in the school, and whose word would go for a good deal. I wonder who it can be? —I hope it isn't Julia."

"No, I don't believe it is. But I want to tell you one thing, Alice; you'd better not say anything to Julia about this listening business. I know

she'd be very angry with you for doing it, and as
likely as not think it was her duty to report you.
Now *I* don't feel so about it, I'm not so strict, you
know. I think it was very natural for you to do it,
and I don't blame you the least in the world.
Little girls will do such things. But Julia would
think it was horrible, she would think you were
disgraced forever, and would make a dreadful row
about it. So, if you take my advice, you'll keep
perfectly quiet. Just tell her what Mrs. Seward
said, and then say you were running down to tell
her when I stopped you to do an errand for me,
and then made you sit down and eat some dough-
balls, and you forgot."

"But," stammered Alice, dropping her dough-
balls, and looking wretchedly frightened, "I didn't
mean to do anything bad. I'll tell Julia I didn't
mean to; she will understand; she won't be
angry."

"She *will* be angry; she said the other night,
listening seemed to her as bad as stealing. You're
a goose if you tell her—a regular goose. There,
don't begin to cry; nobody knows it but me, and *I*
won't tell. Pshaw! it's nothing, except to such
'highfalutin' girls as Julia. I tell you, there's no
harm done. I'm the only one that knows."

"Oh!" cried Alice, in an agony, "there's Julia

waving her handkerchief to me to come. What *shall* I do! Oh, I am so afraid!"

. "Nonsense; pretend you don't see her for a minute, till you get the tears wiped off your cheeks. Now, don't look so scared. Go right up, and tell her all about Mrs. Seward's message, and just hold your tongue about the rest. That's all you've got to do. I'm sure it's simple enough."

"Oh, if the bell would only ring!" groaned Alice.

"Well, it will if you wait a few minutes. Don't look that way; look into the house. Tell me, was there anything more you can remember of what they said?"

"No—oh, no!" said Alice, miserably. "I only wish I hadn't heard anything. I never thought "——

"Just keep it to yourself, that's all. And if you hear anything more about it from anybody, be sure you come straight to me and tell me; do you hear? Then I'll keep *your* secret for you. I won't let Julia or Laura find out that you've been eavesdropping, as long as you tell me everything you hear about Louie, and don't tell anybody else. You understand?"

"Yes," Alice returned, with a deep sigh.

"Now go; and here are the rest of the dough-

balls for you. Wrap 'em up in this paper. There,
put 'em in your pocket, and go to Julia."

Alice put the package into her pocket with a
strange realization, poor little sinner! of the insufficiency of wealth to allay the stings of conscience or
the fears of guilt. She crept down the steps and
across the paved court into the open ground beyond, with a step the very reverse of the one with
which she generally ran to meet her dearest Julia.

Her dearest Julia, now the most wretched of
Julias, had been watching her with an impatience
that threatened at last to get beyond her control.
She had pulled to fragments the delicate apple-
blossoms that the wind had shaken into her lap,
then, pushing them away, had bent with resolution
over her book, and tried to keep her wandering
eyes upon it.

" Oh, if she would only come!" was the sole idea
she found in her mind after she had read twice
through the entire reign of Henry IV.

But when at last she saw a curly little head ap-
pear at the door of the hall, and watched its arrest
and detention by Adelaide McFarlane, and waited
in vain for its release, she had need of all the
patience she had ever learned. A dozen times
she started forward to call Alice to her; but she
had resolved she would wait there for her, and not

stir till she came, and there was a sort of heroism about Julia that made it the most natural and characteristic thing she could do, to wait with outward quietness and suffer inward torture rather than break the shadow of a resolution. She waved her handkerchief to the little loiterer as a sign she waited for her; that unnoticed, she took up her book and read unflinchingly on. She did not even turn her head when she heard Alice's little feet slowly and harassingly brushing through the long grass; she only raised her eyes as she stopped in front of her, and said quietly:

"Well?"

"I'm sorry to have been so long, Julia," Alice began.

"Oh, no matter for that. Did you see Mrs. Seward?"

"Yes, I saw Mrs. Seward, and I was coming right down to tell you only—only "——

"Only Addy stopped you. I know, dear. What did Mrs. Seward say? Sit down, if you're tired, and tell me quietly all you've heard of Louie."

"Why, I've seen Mrs. Seward; I had to wait ever so long, and she says Louie was very ill last night, very ill, indeed "——

"I knew that by her face," Julia said, involuntarily. "Go on."

"Well, Miss Barlow took her to the nursery, and she's there now, and is a little more quiet, and Mrs. Seward says you mustn't be worried, and I am to go at noon to hear again."

"But what does the doctor say? Does Mrs. Seward seem uneasy?"

"I don't know," returned Alice, stupidly. "That's all she told me to tell you."

"I suppose nobody can see her. I suppose there's no chance they'd let me in"——

"I don't know," Alice said again, her eyes wandering absently around.

"Didn't you hear anything else, Ally? Didn't Mrs. Seward say anything about her symptoms? Has she fever?"

"Why, Julia, how should I know?" cried Alice, a little fretfully. "I'm sure I don't know anything about her symptoms. She's sick, that's all I can tell you."

Julia sighed as Alice turned her head restlessly away, exclaiming as she caught sight of a group of girls some distance off:

"Oh, there's Eva Leonard beckoning to me to come play tag. May I go, Julia?"

"Yes, of course you may go," said Julia, sadly; and the little girl bounded off, only too glad to escape the dangerous ground on which Julia threatened to tread.

"How careless and trifling Alice is growing!" thought Julia.

"How strict and cold Julia is!" thought Alice, rushing into Eva Leonard's arms.

The wedge had a very fine point, to be sure—quite invisible to the naked eye; but in this hitherto firm friendship it had been inserted, and one or two skillful blows were only needed to make the separation it would inevitably effect apparent to the parties in the friendship, and the parties who looked on.

CHAPTER XII.

TAG. .

"A light wind chased her on the wing,
  And in the chase grew wild;
As close as might be would he cling
  About the darling child."

TENNYSON.

THE boisterous game in which little Alice was
trying to drown her remorse, soon led the partici-
pators in it to the extreme limits of the playground.
Eva Leonard was "it," and being the best runner
in the school, was giving the flock of girls before
her pretty good work to keep out of her reach. They
had considerably the "head start" or they would
not have had the smallest chance; as it was, one
after another reached "goal" and clung panting to
it, without evincing the least disposition to try the
fortunes of war again; only Susie McAllister, her
face unspeakably red, stood about a hundred yards
from safety, fluctuating between hope and fear,
making frantic attempts to cross, and rushing
breathless back, as Eva's movements indicated that

she meant to give chase. There is no determining
the length of time this exciting little contest con-
sumed, and no measuring the amusement nor the
interest it aroused; it might have been indefinitely
prolonged if Alice Aulay, the catspaw-in-general to
the school, had not, at a sign from Susie, made a
feint of leaving her place, and drawn off Eva's attention, under cover of which Susie ran desperately
across the ground, and touched "goal" with a
shrill, triumphant shriek.

Alice was too little to be "it," so, after giving
her a very provoked shake, Eva released her and
returned to the charge, in not the sweetest frame
of mind, it must be confessed. Her temper
was doomed to a further trial, however, for Sue
McAllister, though she did grow very red in the
face, and did not get over the ground with the same
light grace that distinguished her opponent, made
pretty good time notwithstanding, and husbanded
her strength, and managed some very judicious
moves. The girls laughed provokingly as Eva
again failed in her attempts upon Sue, and they
gained courage themselves to make little sorties
that were inexpressibly exasperating to her, as in
every case where she was unsuccessful, they thought
themselves called upon to laugh more than they
did the time before.

Eva felt that her reputation was at stake; she had been "it" much too long, somebody must be caught; so she watched her chance, and darted suddenly and violently upon Georgy Reynolds, and made a grab at her frock; but Georgy, slight and graceful as a fairy, sprung out of the way, and fled laughing across the lawn, while Eva, too precipitate to be prudent, turned fiercely in pursuit.

In and out among the trees, along the paths, across the lawn, with the eyes of all upon them, the pursued and the pursuer flew, Georgy light, and laughing, and fresh, Eva fagged, and hot, and angry. The time-serving little crew of lookers-on clapped their hands and shouted: "That's it, Georgy!" as the two neared the goal again. They had always before this staked their faith, if not their money, on Eva, but Eva was evidently out of luck to-day, and so, like bigger children, they veered around, and lavished their favor and encouragement on the winning horse.

Perfectly exasperated by all this, as Georgy stretched out her hand, within three feet of the goal, Eva made a sudden and desperate spring, clutched at Georgy, and would have seized her if that young athlete, grasping the pole, had not swung herself around it and landed herself safely on the other side, while her antagonist, disappointed of her mark, missed her footing and fell violently forward. In the *mêlée* that followed, there was a great confusion of condolence and ridicule, while Eva regained her feet and shook the dust from her dress.

"Are you hurt?" somebody asked, as she rubbed off the gravel from her scratched and smarting hands.

"Hurt! I'm not a baby!" she cried, bravely. "Don't stand around me unless you want to be caught."

"Oh, you're worn out. You can't catch anybody."

"You'll see if I can't!"

And clearing the goal, she sent flying before her two or three girls who had unguardedly and idly been looking on. They kept pretty close together, and she drove them down the path, gaining upon them very visibly; but just before she reached them, again her foot slipped, and she fell at full length on the gravel. Gravel isn't a pleasant thing to fall on at any time, but least of all, when the palms, that take the worst of it, are scratched and bleeding from a previous encounter; and Eva, crazy with the pain no less than with the mortification, started up, her southern blood all in a flame, and sprung upon the first person she could grasp.

"You're it," she cried. "Come along."

"No," protested the captive. "Let me go."

"I won't. It's fair. You're it."

"Yes," cried the girls, crowding round. "She caught you, you've got to be it."

"But I'm not playing," the girl said, earnestly.

"Oh, that's very fine to say now you're caught; but it won't do. You shall take your turn. Come, I say."

"Don't—please don't," Frances said, shrinking back. "I never played; I can't. I was walking up and down studying; I didn't see you coming. Let me go, if you please."

"That I won't," muttered Eva, holding the slight wrist of the new-comer in a very tight grasp as she started forward. "You'd no business to get in my way if you didn't mean to play. You knew that was our ground."

"Oh, Eva, let the girl go if she wants to," said Georgy Reynolds. "Don't bully."

Eva snapped a very sharp look at the speaker out of her "double action" eyes, and didn't answer, but dragged her prisoner on with much increased decision of manner.

"Why," cried Eliza Evarts, a lazy West Indian of some hundred and fifty pounds weight, who had never run a race or played a game in her life, but who always hovered on the outskirts of the play ground, lolling around the goal, and watching her companions with interest; "why, she's a good-for-nothing, moping, little baggage, anyhow. It'll be a charity to wake her up. Make her try it, I say."

"Lo! the poor Indian!" cried Addy McFarlane, joining the group, quite unable to resist the temptation of having a finger in such a promising pie. "Make the poor Indian try it, *I* say."

"She'd founder a hundred yards from shore," laughed Georgy.

"She'd go down within sight of land," said another.

"We'll try this slim little craft then this heat," Addy said, laying her hand on Frances' shoulder and leading her forward. "We'll let the poor Indian off this time if she'll promise not to cabbage more than her pocket full of crackers at noon " ——

"Take care," said Eliza. "*I* only do a retail business."

"Come!" cried Addy, letting the suggestion pass unnoticed, and smothering it in an excessive zeal for the continuance of the game. "Why don't you start, girls? Pale-face is waiting."

They were by this time in the middle of the lawn, halfway between the house and the goal. The girls, eager for the game, and specially interested now that it had a spice of malice in it, ranged themselves for a start, and waited only for Adelaide to give the signal. Eva took a good position herself, determined this time not to be outdone; Adelaide held Frances by the arm several yards off, then crying:

"One, two, *three!*" dropped the arm and dashed forward after her flying comrades.

It was not till the foremost one was halfway to the goal, that they were brought to a sudden standstill by Addy's exclamation:

"Heigho! She hasn't started! What's the matter with the girl?"

They paused in mid-career, and turned amazed. Addy went back a few steps and the others followed her, till they closed around the object of their amazement and indignation.

For a second, no one spoke. She looked so white and frightened, with her head drooping and her fingers laced nervously together, that they stood silenced about her, till Addy broke the charm. Whatever pity they had begun to feel for their timid captive, vanished at the first sound of Adelaide's sneering voice.

It makes one blush to think what a single daring girl can do with a crowd of better cómrades. Girls who would shrink from doing an ungentle or ungenerous act individually, will, under the stimulus of excitement, and from the contagion of a bad example, follow an unprincipled leader to incredible lengths of unkindness and cruelty. They will do in a body what they would never dream of doing by themselves. They will persecute miserable teachers, torture homesick girls, resist rules, dare punishments, that as individuals they would quake to think of. Perhaps there was no girl of all that group, with the exception of Adelaide herself, who would have looked with anything like rudeness or unkindness on Frances, from the impulses of her own heart; none who would not have been moved to pity by the sight of her helplessness and unhappiness. But led by the laugh of contempt on Adelaide's face, and her confident tone of assurance, one followed another in joining with her, and when poor little Frances raised her eyes, it was to rest them on a semi-circle of unsympathetic faces, some laughing, some sneering, all curious and cold.

"What do you mean by leading us such a dance?" demanded Adelaide. "Ar'nt you ashamed of yourself for treating your betters so? You ought to be thankful that we'd let you play with us at all. It was a great deal more than you deserved, mean-spirited little thing as you are. You may depend upon it, you'll never get another chance"

"It strikes me it won't be much of a loss, Addy, if it's such a chance as she's just had," said Georgy, with a laugh.

"Well, to be sure, it wasn't a very high compliment," Addy returned, echoing the laugh. "But it is the nearest approach to one she's ever received within my knowledge, and she ought to have been grateful. Come, what have you got to say for yourself, pale-face? Don't stand there so stupid. Tell me why you didn't run; speak, quick."

But Frances did not speak, neither did she raise her head again, and after a moment's impatient pause, some one exclaimed:

"What's to be done? The pretty darling wants to be coaxed—she wants a sugar-plum and a rattle."

"She can't run alone yet!" cried another. "Poor little Toddlekins!"

"What was it its last birthday, dear?"

"Where's nursey?"

"Does its mother know it's out?"

"Is it happy in its mind?"

And a shower of similar scintillations of school-girl sarcasm, the scorching sting of which, none but a school-girl can understand. Indeed, if they had uttered the most innocent and inoffensive combination of words of which the language is capable, they

could not have failed to wound, so apparent was
the spirit that actuated them, and so unmistakable
was the attitude of antagonism they assumed. And
every word was a dagger to the poor child, used to
so few words of any kind from them, shy of the
most commonplace encounter with them, startled
at even an offended look, sensitive beyond the possibility of comprehension among them. To be
standing so before them, the object of all eyes,
would have been misery to her, if she had been an
object of praise and congratulation ; but to be standing before them, at once the centre of aversion and
ridicule, was such unutterable torture that I cannot
hope to make you understand it, if you do not understand her, if you have not in your memory
some one resembling her. Or recall all the shyness
and sensitiveness of which your own childhood bore
the stamp, and multiply it by ten, and it may
help you to imagine what the pain was, that those
thoughtless taunts inflicted on the exquisitely sensitive ears on which they fell.

"Come, 'we pause for a reply,'" cried the
doughty leader. "We shall not let you go till you
apologize and explain. Quick! Tell us why you
didn't run."

"Make her tell you!" said Eliza Evarts, throwing herself down on a bench close by, and leaning

her elbows on her knees. "Don't let the little monkey off. She's too obstinate for anything."

"Oh, I don't mean to, you may be sure," Addy cried, grasping Frances by the wrist. "She shall apologize. She has insulted us all, and we'd be as mean-spirited as she is herself, if we let her off."

That was a light in which they had none of them viewed the subject previously, but since Addy seemed to find it so clear and unmistakable, they yielded to her convictions, and began to think she was in the right decidedly, and they had been insulted and put upon by a self-willed, ill-natured girl, who ought to have been glad to have played with them on any terms. Only Georgy Reynolds dissented, and ran off laughing, saying, it struck her "that the boot was on the other leg." Georgy was too old, and held herself too high, to take much interest in such a petty squabble as this. She had to air her spirits occasionally by a romp with her juniors, but the romp over, she always dropped them very quickly, and returned industriously to graver pursuits, quite ignoring any further interest in or responsibility about those she had been amusing herself with for the hour.

"The bell 'll ring in a minute," cried some one in the group.

"Yes," Addy said, "and if you don't want to be

carried straight to Miss Stanton, and complained
of for making a disturbance in the play-ground,
you'd better speak and say you're ashamed of yourself, and ask our pardon."

"I don't believe she's a bit ashamed.   She don't
look so."

"Oh, I'll tell you.   She's such a little saint, perhaps she thinks it's wicked to play tag."

"Do you, sweetheart?"

"Yes!—Yes!   She puts down her head.   She
means yes."

"Ah! that's it, is it?" cried Addy.   "She affects
the pious, does she?   She don't take after that precious sister of hers, then, if I remember right."

"Leave me alone—let go my hand," escaped
Frances' lips in a low, agonized voice, as she made
a sudden struggle to get free.

"What a temper the little vixen has!" cried
Addy, grasping, with all her might, and even then
hardly retaining, the slender wrist that till that
moment had lain quite passive in her hold.   "No,
I shan't let you go till you beg pardon of us all.
You shan't stir till you tell us you're ashamed."

A crimson flush had started to the girl's face,
and her eyes had a hunted, desperate look as she
raised them for an instant to her persecutors ;. then
averting them as if she could not bear the blaze of

contempt they met, she made a sudden spring to break away, uttered a sharp cry of pain as the wrist was twisted violently in Adelaide's unrelenting hand, and fell, white and fainting, at her feet.

"Good heavens! what have I done!" Adelaide exclaimed involuntarily, turning pale as she stooped over the senseless, prostrate figure.

There was a sudden hush among the girls and a frightened look on every face as they crowded closer round her.

"She's fainted dead away. You must have dislocated her wrist. Oh, Adelaide!"

"What shall I do!" and Adelaide put her hand to her head with a look of alarm and indecision.

"How awfully she looks!" whispered Alice, hiding her face and beginning to cry. "Oh, will she die?"

"You ought to be ashamed of yourself, Adelaide," said some one. "You are so rough; you may have killed her."

"Poor girl," murmured one, too late repentant; and in an instant, the contagion of pity spread.

"Something must be done," Eva cried, starting forward. "Somebody rub her hands, and Conny, go as fast as you can to the kitchen for some water, while I run for Mrs. Seward."

"You shan't do anything of the kind," cried

Adelaide, springing after her, recovering her self-
possession. "You shan't bring Mrs. Seward here
till I tell you. Go for the water, Constance. The
girl's only fainted; she'll come to in a second.
And let me tell you, once for all, it's no more my
fault than it is yours, and if you tell Mrs. Seward
so, you'll every one of you find reason to wish you
hadn't, before the week is over."

"I'd like to know how it's anybody's fault but
yours," Eliza Evarts said.

"You've all been bullying and teasing her, every
one here, and you know it perfectly well. I
haven't said anything more than any one else "——

"Yes, but you've *done* more—you've sprained
her wrist."

"I haven't, 'twas her own doing; she wrenched
her hand away so quick; how could I know what
she was about?"

"Settle that among yourselves," cried Eva,
breaking away from her. "I'm going for Mrs.
Seward."

And before Adelaide could answer, she was half-
way across the lawn toward the house. Meanwhile,
the frightened girls knelt around their companion
with momentarily increasing alarm. She did not
come to in the least, or show the smallest sign of
returning consciousness, for all their efforts. They

chafed her hands and feet, and poured the water that Constance came running back with, on her temples, but she lay as white and still as marble. There was hardly a word spoken; they were too miserable and penitent now to quarrel and accuse each other, and even Adelaide moved aside with a feeling of relief to make way for Mrs. Seward, who came hurrying toward them, accompanied by Eva.

"What is all this?" she cried, stooping down and touching Frances' pulse. "Fainted quite away! My poor little girl!"

And without a moment's indecision, lifting the light burden in her arms, she laid the death-like face gently against her shoulder, and hurried toward the house.

CHAPTER XIII.

FRANCES.

"Heaven is of souls the native sphere,
O heaven-born soul, live stranger here."

BISHOP KEN.

"LAURA, wait for me a minute; the bell hasn't stopped yet," said Julia, uneasily, lingering by the foot of the stairs.

"What are you waiting for?" and Laura paused. "I always like to be early at the noon-service, it's so short."

"Yes, I know—so do I," she returned, making a movement to go, but loitering and looking wistfully up the stairs. "I've been hoping Mrs. Seward would come out. I don't like to knock at the nursery door for fear of disturbing Louie, but I'd give anything to know how she is."

"Maybe Miss Stanton will be in Chapel, and she'll be sure to know; or any of the teachers will go up and inquire for you if you ask them, or give you permission to go in."

196

"Very well;" and as the bell stopped, the two
friends walked slowly away.

At this moment, they heard the nursery door
open, and Julia started and looked back. But it
was only Frances Chenilworth, who with a slow and
languid step descended the stairs, and crossed the
hall toward the passage that led to the Chapel.
Her arm was in a sling, and she looked white and
ill. Laura and Julia paused to wait for her, and
the former said, as she approached them:

"I didn't think you'd be well enough to come
down, Frances. I am so sorry to hear you've hurt
your wrist so badly."

"Thank you," and Frances flushed faintly. "I
am better; it wasn't very bad. Mrs. Seward gave
me permission to come down to Chapel."

"You're not going into school to-day?"

"Oh, no."

"Can you tell me," said Julia, hesitatingly,
"whether Louie Atterbury is better? Did you see
her?"

"Oh, yes. I've been sitting by her since eleven
o'clock. I believe they think she's better—at least,
the doctor does. Mrs. Seward doesn't say much,
but I think it worries her that the fever keeps so
high. But she thought it was a good sign when
Louie knew me."

"Why! is she delirious?"

"Yes. She has not recognized anybody before; and even now, though she makes me sit by her and keep hold of her hand, I don't think half the time she thinks it's me."

"Oh, Frances! I had no idea it was as bad as that."

"Very likely she'll be better when she wakes up. She's dozing now."

They separated at the Chapel door, and each one went to her accustomed seat. Julia, as she rose from her knees, took up Louie's worn and ill-used little Prayer-book, that lay on the bench as she had laid it down last night. Poor Louie! it might be long before she could come to Chapel again. Julia missed her sorely, though they had been so much separated of late. She began to see how fond she was of her—how much more she cared for her than for any one else. Laura, so beautiful and good, did not fill Louie's place in her heart; nor Miss Emily, perfect as she believed her to be, nor Alice, pet and darling as she had always been; nobody could fill Louie's place—reckless, heedless, self-willed Louie. This was no time or place to remember her faults or her unkindnesses. Julia only remembered her honesty and spirit, and the generous and unselfish love she had so long shown for her.

She only remembered her own share in the mis-understandings that had given them both so much pain—her .own pride and reserve and want of gentleness. Oh! if she could only see her for a moment—only ask her to forgive her; she never could be happy till she did. She could not bear to think of her, lying there suffering and ill, while she was well and strong; poor Louie! not able even to say her prayers, perhaps—not able to say a word to defend herself from the accusations of her enemies, or the wrong judgments of her friends.

There were not very many in Chapel that day, indeed, the mid-day service was never very largely attended. It was a voluntary service, and took up more than half of the short recess allowed at noon, and between the demands of study, and the desire for recreation, but a small proportion of the large school found their way into the quiet Chapel. But to those who did, it was the sweetest service of the day—a lull in its busy turmoil—a momentary break in the business and pleasure that none are too young to find engrossing—a respite and refresh-ment that none ever failed to find the benefit of. The teachers, the older girls, the communicants, and a few stragglers, generally formed the number. Louie almost always came; why, she could hardly have told. Very often, before twelve o'clock, she thought she would dispose otherwise of her recess, either resolving to have a romp in the grounds with some of the rompingly inclined, or a quiet half-hour in the schoolroom to look over her afternoon lessons, or a few stolen minutes to increase the voluminous weekly letter to her mother; but somehow, before the bell stopped ringing, Louie would find herself putting away books and portfolios, and almost involuntarily following her graver companions into Chapel. It was not exactly because she liked it, though she could not help being soothed by the quiet of the hour and service; neither did she look upon it altogether in the light of a duty; she had neglected greater duties, and was continuing to neglect them. But she had a vague feeling that she was missing something that was offered to her, when she turned her back upon a holy service; that it was recorded against her, if her place was vacant when two or three gathered together in His name, insured the fulfillment of the promise; that she lost a blessing when she yielded to indolence or to pleasure or to profit, and stayed away. In short, she did not dare to do it.

Very misty, undefined and crude her notions were perhaps; superstitious, very likely, and in a way incorrect. But maybe they were better than a good deal of the enlightenment that one some-

times sees in older and wiser people, an enlightenment of which one cannot but feel the coldness and
insufficiency, when tested by the requirement,
" Except ye become as little children ;"—for the
Kingdom we are all striving, or pretending to
strive, to enter into, can hold no selfish heart, no
half-way sacrifice, no unconquered ambition, no
uncrucified affection—only the utter love of loving
children, the simple faith of believing children, the
self-renunciation of dutiful children, the prostrate
reverence, if you will, of superstitious children.
God Himself will enlighten all such ignorance, will
make theirs a more "perfect day" for the clouds of
humility that have hung about the dawn ; will exalt
them none the less for having abased themselves.

And, sooner or later, outside the gate of that
Kingdom, that lesson must be learned, that self-
abasement must be made. Happy they who learn
it at the outset, whose path, however weary, is
lighted from above, whose burden, whatever it may
be, is not self-imposed and fruitless, but sent, with
strength to bear it, from One who pities them as a
father pitieth his own children.

Little Frances Chenilworth had " learned that
sacrifice;" more than any other, perhaps, she had
got rid of pride and love of self, and had got
instead of it, the love of God, and the holiness that

it brings into the soul. Sweet little saint, she had
died unto the world so utterly that now it almost
ceased to tempt her; she was so far above it that
its vexations and its allurements scarcely reached
her heaven-tuned ear, seldom drew down her
heaven-charmed eye.

"Did you ever notice what a sweet face that
Chenilworth girl has?" whispered Laura Boutwell
to Julia as they came out of Chapel. "I looked
at her during service, and I am sure I never saw
anything lovelier; look at her now—no, it's all
gone. She's so different when you speak to her, or
when any one is looking at her."

"Do you know," said Julia, "it sometimes
strikes me that we've been very careless about her?
Don't you think she'd like to be friends with
some of us? She seems so lonely, it worries
me."

"She's so shy, how can one get friends with her.
Just watch her now, shrinking out of sight and
stealing back to the nursery. There! Miss Stanton sees her, and has stopped her. Poor little mite,
how miserable she looks, blushing and scared at the
least word. How odd it must be to be so afraid of
people."

"What can Miss Stanton be saying to her, to
make her so nervous. She can't be scolding her,

the teachers never scold her. I wish it weren't wrong to go near enough to hear."

Julia's scruples were soon settled by Miss Stanton, who turned toward them and called them to her. She laid her hand kindly on Frances' shoulder as she said:

"Can either of you help this little girl in telling me about what occurred in the playground this morning? I want to understand how she came to be so great a sufferer in the affair. She is not generally boisterously inclined, I think, and it seems odd to me that she should have met with such a severe accident from her own carelessness. Were you out in the grounds at the time, Laura?"

"It was my hour for practising, ma'am. I was in the house all the morning."

"I was there, Miss Stanton," Julia said, as Miss Stanton turned interrogatively toward her. "I was studying, but the girls were playing a good way off, and I didn't know anything of what had happened till I saw Mrs. Seward hurrying out, and I followed her, and found that Frances had fainted."

"Frances, do you often play tag, child? Do you love to romp?"

Frances' head was in that particular attitude that the top of it alone was visible; and that

portion being the least expressive of the entire sur
face, it followed that Miss Stanton was not much
enlightened by her study of it. Neither was
there much to be gained from the faint, incoherent
responses that her inquiries elicited, so with a shake
of the head, she said, as she dismissed them:

"I see Frances does not mean to tell me what I
want to know, but I am sure it will come out some
way."

"Tell me," said Julia, in a low tone, following
her to the stairs " wasn't Adelaide teasing you?
Wasn't it her fault? I know it was."

"Oh don't—please don't!" and Frances turned
toward her with a look of entreaty. "If you only
knew how wretched it makes me to be asked, you
wouldn't do it yourself, nor let the others do it. I
don't mind about the pain—it's no matter how it
happened—why *will* they tease me when it don't
make any difference to them how it happened. I
am so afraid they'll make me tell. They'll know I
dare not disobey."

"They won't if they know you're so unhappy
about it," said Julia, earnestly. "Nobody could
have the heart to be severe with you; I know Miss
Stanton couldn't, she likes you better than any of
us. Depend upon it, she won't ask you another
word, now she's seen how you feel about it. I'm

sure I'll do all I can to hush it up, and keep the girls from plaguing you with questions; and don't be afraid of hearing anything about it, if you are well enough to come into class to-morrow. Sit by me, won't you?"

"Thank you."

"And Laura likes you so much, it would be so nice if you would walk with us on the bank some times!"

"You're very kind."

"But you will, won't you? I am sure we should be good friends, I've often thought so in Chapel. And since you like Louie too, it seems as if I knew you better. You can't think how much I miss her. You don't really think she's very sick?"

"I don't know, I'm not much used to seeing sick people; I hope not, but anyhow, she's very miserable, and I'm very sorry for her."

"Frances, I'd give anything to go in and see her."

"Wouldn't Mrs. Seward let you, don't you think?"

"If you would only ask her"——

"Come then, before the bell rings;" and Julia followed Frances to the nursery door, and stood anxiously waiting outside it, while she went in to beg the desired permission. There was a whispered consultation, and then Mrs. Seward came

out, and Julia read her sentence in her kind, pitying face.

"I am so sorry, my dear child!" she said, taking
her hand. "I can understand how you feel, and I
wish it were right to let you see Louie for a little
while; but, you see, she is in just that state that
any excitement might do her a great deal of harm.
The doctor said, an hour ago, that no one had better be about her but myself, and little Frances, who
is soft and quiet as a shadow, and by whom Louie
seems most easily soothed; so I have sent the nurse
away, and do not mean to have any one else in the
room, unless I find it necessary at night. I confess
this is an anxious day with me, but I trust by
to-morrow there will be such an improvement
as will set all our fears at rest. Don't look so distressed, my child—I may exaggerate; the doctor is
not alarmed as yet. This is a sudden attack, but
she is strong and young —— There! Oh, why
will they ring the bell so loud! Run down, dear,
and tell them not to come in this part of the hall,
the next half-hour."

The bells rang cruelly to Julia's ears, though,
after that, even in the furthest extremity of the
hall, and the girls laughed cruelly loud and carelessly; for her own heart, muffled in its great dread,
trembled even at its own quick beating.

CHAPTER XIV.

GATHERING GLOOM.

"In face of a great sorrow like to death,
  How do we wrestle night and day with tears;
  How do we fast and pray; how small appears
  The outside world, while, hanging on some breath
  Of fragile hope, the chamber where it lies
  Includes all space."

MISS MULOCH.

BEFORE noon the next day, it was known all over the school that Louie Atterbury was very ill—so ill, indeed, that there had been two doctors upstairs half the morning, that Mrs. Seward never left her bedside, and that prayers had been said for her in Chapel. There was a hush over everything. No bells were rung throughout the house, and the teachers, grave and silent, checked the slightest noise or hurry in going from class to class. You would hardly have known it for the same place as yesterday, if you had been there at the noon recess. There were three times as many girls in Chapel as there had been the day before, and when they came out, though most of them collected in groups about the hall, and talked, it was in such low, serious tones that they hardly sounded like school-girls' tones at all.   There was little or no playing going on anywhere about the grounds.   Some of the younger ones were trying to sustain a game of hide-and-seek below the apple-trees, but it soon languished, and one after another fell off, and straggled back to the house, and hung about the skirts of their elders in the hall, and listened to the talking that was going on.

For indeed there was a good deal to talk about just then—a good deal to excite the wonder of the curious and the regret of the well-disposed.   Besides the natural depression caused by the dangerous illness of their young companion, who, with all her faults, had been, in a certain way, of consequence among them, and was more missed than many a better girl would have been, there had come out some circumstances that roused their interest very keenly, and produced many conflicting opinions.   For little Alice Aulay, as was to be supposed, had not been able to hold her tongue, and all that Adelaide's threats effected, had been, in her great remorse and alarm at the sight of Julia's sorrow, to make her blurt out, before all the dormitory, all she knew of poor Louie's case, and all her own penitence for

listening, in such a very unequivocal way, that in a
few hours the whole story became school talk.

It was a story that those who were in authority
would fain, just now, have kept quiet. It was very
painful to judge harshly of the poor girl who lay
just trembling between life and death; it was very
frightful to believe the worst of her; and there
was no one, from Miss Barlow up, who would
not thankfully have put the case out of sight at
once, and till there was some change, have let it
rest entirely. But this the little tattler had made
impossible by her disclosures; and Louie's rebellion,
disobedience, falsehood, were discussed, in all their
bearings, from the Primary to Senior A. Nothing
else was thought of, nothing else was talked of. No
efforts now to suppress the tale could have proved
at all effectual, and the only way was to let things
take their course, leaving it to time to clear all up,
and hoping always for the best.

Adelaide McFarlane paid more than one visit to
the Study, but she knew how to hold her tongue,
if Alice did not; and all that her companions had
to judge from, of the nature of her interviews, was
the unusual paleness of her face and nervousness of
her manner, when she came out. Adelaide, indeed,
was very far from being happy or comfortable. It
was something very much like remorse that made

her wish, now Louie lay so beyond her power, that she could own all, and get it off her conscience. But she had gone too far for that; she was so tangled up in her own deceits that she dared not attempt to extricate herself. The only thing she could do was to shut her eyes to all thoughts of repentance, and go on as she had begun. She tried to say to herself confidently, that Louie would get well, and then what a fool she would have made of herself for nothing! No, she would not for a moment allow herself to think there was any real danger of her dying. If there had been, why of course she wouldn't have dared to let them go on thinking as they now thought about the novel. She hadn't told Miss Barlow that Louie was reading it, she hadn't told a lie about anything. She'd only said, Louie had brought back a good many books to school with her, and so she had.

And, in all the cross-questionings she had to go through in the Study, she escaped without telling any flagrant falsehood—without saying anything for which she could not find an excuse for herself and a palliation afterward, when she reviewed her conduct. Her standing in the school was very fair; her word, as yet, had never been doubted, so that her testimony, faint, evasive as it was, went a good way toward strengthening the conviction of

Louie's guilt, that pervaded most minds. The teachers, almost all, were obliged to own to themselves that there was very little room left them for doubt; and the girls, though at first they had exclaimed against the possibility of Louie Atterbury's untruthfulness, had, one by one, come round to view the case, as, indeed, it seemed impossible not to view it. How could they help believing what was so clear—what, in fact, everybody believed?

It was very sad; it was terrible to think that she was so near eternity with such a sin upon her soul, and without the power to repent of it; unconscious of her danger—insensible alike to fear and sorrow. Even the most thoughtless were in a degree subdued by this; it was better than ten sermons, to remind them how near Death might be to every one of them—how stealthy in his approach he was, and how much it behooved them that that approach should not surprise them in sin. Even the most careless grew pale as they remembered how few hours ago it was that the girl who now lay dying, perhaps, had romped with the wildest among them —had been as careless as they, and thought her hold on life just as secure. The teachers did not fail to impress this lesson, and began to hope, seeing the impression made, that good would be brought out of all this seeming evil, and from poor

Louie's sin and sudden punishment might be snatched a mercy for her thoughtless comrades.

But, in the meantime, had none any faith left in her? Now that she lay upstairs in the hushed and darkened nursery, as unconscious of past or present as if she had entered, instead of neared, the dark valley, had all resigned all care for her, all belief in her uprightness? Her high spirit was brought down so low, her clever brain was so clouded with the stupor of fever, her words were but the faint and incoherent murmurs of delirium —it seemed cruel that she should be left to defend herself—that those who had so readily shared her affection in times of health, should desert her in this her hour of need. Poor child. Perhaps though, after all, it mattered little to her then; the truest and tenderest friend can go but a little way on the gloomy road on which she seemed entering, there is but one sort of Love that can avail much then,

"Since all alone, so Heaven has willed, we die."

But all had not forgotten; little Frances night and day beside her, and Julia, night and day with a prayer for her on her trembling lips and in her aching heart, had not forgotten and could not forget. Never for a moment had Julia believed her

guilty; anything else would have been easier to
have supposed her capable of; Julia knew her truth
and honesty too well. But how could she defend
her? How could she convince them against their
own senses, against what seemed so certain? Reserved and shy at all times—she was doubly so
now, with the weight of this dread about her, the
stifling, choking terror that this, her first actual
approach to real grief, inspired her with. It was so
bewildering and so awful to think that Louie might
die. She had thought more about death than most
girls of her age, she knew how suddenly it had
come to many, how suddenly it might come to her,
but she was as much astounded, as much stunned,
when she met its actual advance, as we all, wise as
well as foolish, always are. It can never strike
such terror the second time, it may come in a worse
form, and deal as deep a blow; but we know somewhat of the pain we are to bear; we are half
familiar with the suffering, we know it is but death
after all. But at first, the awful uncertainty, the
newness, the strangeness, the unsettling of all on
which we have always leaned, the sudden darkness
to eyes used only to morning light; what pain is
there like this?

Julia had no word of defence when she heard her
companions whispering over Louie's trouble; even

when Laura shook her head sadly, and said she hated to believe it, but there seemed no help; she could only say :

"You need not believe it, Laura. You ought to know her better—she never, never did it—you will all know some day, I am sure—you will all be sorry enough."

As for Frances, she had little chance to know anything of what was going on outside the nursery. She knew but vaguely of the story that engaged the interest of her school-mates so strongly, for even after she was well enough herself to go down-stairs, she had not the heart to leave Louie, who had clung to her so tenaciously. Now, alas! she was beyond even the bewildered recognition she had then shown, but Frances could not bear to go, and had begged so earnestly of Mrs. Seward that she might be allowed to remain and watch her, that the kind-hearted matron had not been able to steel herself into refusing. Indeed, few people ever refused Frances anything; the teachers, one and all, treated her with the extremest gentleness and consideration, and she was now allowed to do, what to no one else, perhaps, would have been per-mitted.

How often now Frances thought of their talk in Miss Emily's room; she clung as a last hope, to what Louie had then said. It may seem strange, but Frances did not think there was anything terrible in dying; if she had been sure of one thing about Louie, perhaps she would have envied her. If she had not known that Louie had failed to prepare herself for death, she would not have looked upon what now gave her so much dread, as anything worse than a short parting from one she had begun to love.

But to think that she might never be conscious again, never have a moment to repent, never have grace to say a prayer, never be able to receive the Sacrament she had neglected, this was what filled her with such dread as the hope of Louie's life waxed fainter and fainter. She did not know what the girls downstairs knew; she only thought of that one thing, and prayed for the saving of her companion's soul—while the rest prayed—as we all pray, showing by our earnestness that the frail body comes first in our esteem.

When prayers were said for Louie, Julia's heart almost died within her at the last clause of the petition; she could hardly submit to say it, but to Frances, it was the most vital part of all, and the part on which her earnestness was spent.

There is not any need of prolonging a sad story, on Saturday afternoon (the longest, saddest Satur-

day that any one ever remembered at St. Mary's),
it was known throughout the school that all hope
was over, the doctors had said there was no longer
any, Louie could hardly live till night. Miss Emily had come downstairs crying, and no one had
dared to ask her anything, they all knew too well
what it meant; but going into the school-room
where most of the girls were sitting, she had made
an effort to tell them the sad news, and then, covering her face with her handkerchief, leaned sobbing against a desk.

There was a moment's silence, and then low sobs
and broken ejaculations were heard, as the awe-
struck children began to realize the truth. Two or
three clung weeping around their teacher, others
older and more self-controlled, remained in their
seats, with hardly any outward show of emotion, but
with none the less of genuine sorrow. Only one,
hastily starting up, left the room; it was Adelaide
McFarlane.

"Don't, oh Julia, don't, my darling!" sobbed little
Alice on her knees with her head in Julia's lap.
"Oh, don't stare so—don't look so dreadfully!
Miss Emily, tell her not—Julia—Julia, look at me
—*won't* you speak to me!"

"Children," said Miss Emily raising her head
and trying to command her voice, "I want to tell

you something else, something I am very thankful to have to tell you. You know how I have dreaded, how we all have dreaded, that poor Louie would never be conscious of her state; but about an hour ago, it became evident that consciousness had returned—she recognized Frances, who was beside her, and appeared perfectly herself. It was thought best, as her time for preparation was so short, to tell her the worst immediately. She was dreadfully overcome, poor child, at first, but in a few moments asked to see the Bishop, who had been by her nearly all day and who had only left her an hour before.

And children, I have seen him—just now, as he came out from the nursery. He is sure of one thing, and we must be sure he knows, that dear Louie is fit for the holy rite he means to administer. They dare not put it off any later, so he is coming back at six, to confirm her, and administer the holy communion. Let me add one thing—though it is painful to touch on it ever so slightly at such a time as this. The Bishop has the firmest confidence in the integrity of your companion, and his judgment will have the greatest weight with you I know, and will be the greatest comfort to you. Whatever sad doubts we may have had before, I need not say, should be put out of our minds

now. Let the poor child, whose moments are so
few, have all our prayers, and all our tenderest
thoughts."

That was a solemn hour. The afternoon sun was
sinking rapidly, and the hands of the school-room
clock were approaching six. The house was very
still; Miss Wells had taken the younger children
all out to walk, and the older ones, by common,
though tacit consent, had remained together in the
school-room.

"It was like church," Alice Aulay whispered,
seeking refuge at last with Eva Leonard; for Julia
sat so still, her face so deadly white and her hands
so cold, that the little girl was awed and uncomfortable. She had refused to leave her side when
the other children had gone out to walk, and had
clung around her for a long while. But Julia had
taken no notice of her caresses, had seemed almost
unconscious of them; and little Alice, as the shock
of Miss Emily's news began to wear away, wished
heartily that she had not stayed at home. Why
hadn't she gone with the others? It was so dreadful here, the girls all crying and everything so still,
Julia so wretched and nobody to speak a word to.

By and by she slid down from her seat, and crept
slowly and softly over to Eva Leonard.

Eva sat at the extreme end of the school-room,

her desk was by the last window, and her chair against the closets that ran across the apartment. She was leaning her head against the window, her eyes very red with crying, when she saw Alice coming toward her. She made a place for her beside her, and passed her arm affectionately around her waist, stooping down and whispering a few kind words in her ear.

Poor little Alice felt her terror very much thawed by the warm-hearted Eva's sympathy, and presently was emboldened to ask her if she hadn't any pictures in her desk that she might look at. Eva softly raised the lid of her desk and looked, but she found upon investigation that there was not anything at all picturesque in it. She made an interrogatory gesture toward her slate, but Alice shook her head. Slates savored too much of subtraction, into which rule she had recently entered, and which she entirely loathed; it would be worse than sitting still to play with what had been but yesterday instruments of torture.

"I'll tell you," whispered Eva, "you shall put my work-box in order for me, and I'll give you the empty spools."

Alice brightened, said yes, and taking the workbox in her lap, slid off the chair, and seated herself Turkish fashion on the floor at Eva's feet. She emptied the contents of the box in her lap, and with a very feminine sense of enjoyment began its rearrangement and restoration to order. The amusement was not a short-lived one, she made the most of every item, bestowed much care and thought upon the proper securing of ends in the matter of floss silk and spool cotton, and made great capital of a hank of tangled thread that she had found jammed down in one of the partitions. But the most faithfully nursed job must end at length, and Alice could find no more to do, so lifting the open box up in her hands to Eva, she asked her if it would do.

Eva said, "Yes, indeed, it looked beautifully," it hadn't looked so nicely since she came back to school.

"What shall I do with these snips and papers?" whispered Alice showing a handful of rubbish in her apron.

"Oh, I don't know. Perhaps you'd better run down and put them in the dust-bin."

"I can't, I hate to go out of the school-room; they'll all look at me so. Can't you throw 'em out of the window?"

"No, I had a dreadful scolding last week for throwing papers into the yard. I daren't do it."

"Oh, look here Eva!" and Alice became ener

getic in manner. "Can't I throw 'em into the closet here? There's a lot of rubbish in it already, nobody uses it."

"I suppose you can," Eva said, carelessly. "It doesn't signify."

Eva thought it didn't signify, but in a strange sort of a way, it *did* signify. She turned her face away, and leaning again against the frame of the window, looked listlessly out. The beautiful afternoon sunshine lay golden on the trees and grass, but no one had the heart to enjoy it now. The slanting shadows told that the sunshine was going; and the darkness that fell after it—how long it would be to poor Louie! The thoughts that this suggested made Eva lean down on the desk and put her hands before her face.

Presently she was roused by Alice, who pulled her dress and whispered, "Look what I've found. Did you know it was there?"

Eva said "no, dear," and only glanced indifferently at the dusty, ink-stained book that Alice held up toward her. Alice, very much interested, clambered into the chair she had before vacated, and leaning on her elbows on the desk, spelled over the title page of the volume, and dusted it with the wrong side of her white apron.

"Just look, please, Eva," she said at length, put

ling her companion's sleeve. "Can you make out the name here on the blank leaf? L—— L——, isn't that meant for an L? I wish I could read writing."

Eva, too good natured to neglect the little girl, made an effort to attend to her, and stooping over the book said absently, hardly knowing what had been the child's question:

"Who does the book belong to, dear? I don't know anything about it."

"Why there's a name in it; see if you can read it."

Eva's attention needed no further rousing, for she had caught sight of the name on the first blank leaf:

"LOUIE ATTERBURY—FROM HER MOTHER."

" Poor Louie!" thought Eva, as the tears rushed into her eyes.

"Whose is it? What makes you cry?" demanded Alice.

"Oh, Alice! it's Louie's book—dear Louie's; I wonder how it came there. Did you find it in the bottom of the closet?"

"Yes, ever so far back, and there was a piece of paper all covered with ink too, and a stained pocket-handkerchief: see, there's the handkerchief."

Alice shook the dust off of it and handed it to Eva. "There's a name in the corner," she said.

Though the pocket-handerchief was soaked with ink, there was just enough of one corner clear to let the name be distinguised:

"A. McFARLANE."

"I wonder how *that* came there." And Eva paused perplexed. Her few moments of deliberation resulted in a determination to take the book and handkerchief to Miss Emily, who was sitting at the raised desk in the centre of the room. Beside her sat Miss Barlow, who had just come in, and Laura and Georgy were standing by them, talking in whispers. Going softly down the room, Eva approached the desk, and leaning over it, said:

"Miss Emily, look at this book. It has poor Louie's name in it; Alice found it in the closet, below there."

Miss Emily stretched out her hand for it. "From her mother," she read in an unsteady voice —"Her poor mother little dreams"——

Miss Barlow with a very pale face, bent nervously down to read the name.

"How came it in the closet?" she asked, huskily.

"I don't know—here's a handkerchief of Adelaide McFarlane's that was with it. Alice says "——

"There comes the Bishop," said Georgy in a low tone, glancing out of the window. "Is it six yet?"

The school-room clock that moment began striking. Eva sat down at the platform at Miss Emily's feet, and Georgy leaned her head on Laura's shoulder, whispering:

"I wish they'd let us go into Chapel. It seems as if we ought to be there—praying with them upstairs."

It was so extremely still, every one in the schoolroom heard the Bishop as he left the study and passed through the hall, and upstairs to the nursery. Not many minutes of such silence elapsed, when, with hardly movement and noise enough to break it, Frances Chenilworth entered at the open door. She put her hand a moment before her eyes as if the light hurt them, then came down the room.

She looked paler than ever, and there was a strange, solemn light in her eyes, as if she had been away from earth. No one could have defined it, but every one felt it, and watched her with a sort of reverence.

How different from the day when she had shrunk in terror from their gaze. She had forgotten all about it, if they had not.

"I have come for Julia," she said, in her clear simple voice. "Louie wants her."

"Julia, dear," said Miss Emily, going up to where she sat, her face bowed in her hands, trembling violently. "Julia, do you hear what Frances says? Will you go?"

She raised her head, and making a great effort to control herself, arose slowly and took Frances' offered hand.

"Wait one moment," Miss Emily said quickly. "Frances, here's a book of Louie's that has just been found. Do you suppose it can be the one— the one she has been talking about since she has been sick?"

"The little 'Sacra Privata' her mother gave her? Yes—oh, I am so glad!"

"It was found, Frances, in such an odd place, in the lower part of that closet at the head of the room, all stained as you see, with ink, and a handkerchief and a piece of paper soaked with ink, thrown in with it."

There was a moment's pause. Frances turned thoughtfully the pages of the book as she said:

"Have you asked Adelaide about it?"

"No—what do you know of it? Can Adelaide tell me how it came there."

"I don't know—yes—that is—I saw her throw

something inky into that closet a week or ten days
ago—one morning when I was studying down there
at my desk. I don't know, though; perhaps it
wasn't this—I didn't see what it was—only I heard
something fall in among the papers in the closet,
and when I looked around, I saw her shutting the
door, and her hands were stained with ink; but it
may have been something else."

"No, Frances, you must be right, her name was
on the handkerchief that Alice found with it.
Come with me—I will take this up myself to the
Bishop."

"I wonder where Adelaide is, all this while,"
ejaculated Eva as the others left the room.

CHAPTER XV.

" See'st thou the eastern dawn,
Hearest thou in the red morn
The angels' song ?
O lift thy drooping head,
Thou who in gloom and dread
Hast lain so long.

Death comes to set thee free,
O meet him cheerily
As thy true friend,
And all thy fears shall cease
And in eternal peace,
Thy penance end."

AT the nursery door they paused ; "Wait till you are quieter," said Frances, uneasy at the shuddering grasp that Julia kept upon her hand.

"She will feel better when she sees her," said Miss Emily, soothingly. "It is only the strangeness of it all that unnerves her so. Remember, Julia dear, it is nothing so terrible for Christians, it is only a short parting. Louie has prepared herself—you will, I know, try to help her, and do nothing to increase her agitation."

227

" I am ready—go on, Frances," whispered Julia.

" And, Frances, ask the Bishop to come out a moment and speak to me. I will not detain him long."

The Bishop passed them on the threshold. Julia clung more tightly to Frances' hand as the door closed upon them and they stood within the room. But there was such a peaceful look about everything—the quiet order of the furniture, the Communion Service on the table near the bed, and such a soft, calm light coming in through the windows open to the river, that, unconsciously, she was soothed.

" Is it Julia? Hasn't she come yet?"

Miss Stanton leaning over the pillar, said " Yes, dear," and beckoned Julia to come to the bed. Julia let go Frances' hand, and hesitatingly approached; the patient head upon the pillow turned toward her, and stretching out her arms, Louie said her name.

Julia stooped down toward her, and for a moment there was such a troubled, wistful look in Louie's eyes as she put her arms around her neck.

" Oh Julia!" she whispered; " have they told you? I can't get well—I am going to die—I try not to be frightened—it seems so strange—Oh! I— I am so "——

Julia had sunk on her knees beside the bed, and covering her face, tried in vain to smother her sobs.

"Don't cry so—oh, Julia!" whispered Louie, faintly. "Only tell me you forgive me all the hateful things I've done to you. I know you won't think of them ever again, will you? I know it—but just say so—just say you don't mind."

"Oh, Louie! Louie! I'd give the world if we could live over the last few weeks!"

"But we can't—we can only be sorry. We're friends now, arn't we?"

Friends? Yes, that close embrace meant they were friends; friendship is never so sweet as when the frost of death has touched it. Poor children; they cried and whispered a few more broken confessions and endearments, and then a faintness came over Louie, and Miss Stanton had to lead Julia away, and leave her by the window to recover her composure, while the others bent anxiously over the bed.

The faintness, however, was but of a short duration; Louie soon opened her eyes, and though every moment showed its sure decrease of vitality and color, there was yet strength and vigor enough left to make it almost incredible that her moments of life were indeed so nearly numbered. Her mind was perfectly clear now; it was evident she knew what lay before her, and would not lose one of the few moments that remained to her.

The troubled look that had come into her face when the meeting with Julia had brought up so strongly all her ties to life, had passed away, and in its place, an earnest, solemn light filled her eyes, not altogether peaceful, but faithful, patient, obedient. The coming struggle was uncertain in its length and fierceness, the armor was all untried and new, the clouds that hung over the battle-ground were dark and lurid; but the heart of the young soldier, though sinking sometimes with a deadly fear, owned no rebellion, and no disloyal cowardice. True to duty, relying on Him who had promised, utterly obedient and unmurmuring, she prepared herself for the dismal conflict with the " powers of darkness;" and the only strength that can prevail against them, was made perfect in her weakness.

Some time passed before the door opened, and the Bishop reëntered the room; a faint sigh of relief escaped her lips as he approached. She looked to him so eagerly and wistfully for comfort, that it must almost have pained him to meet her eyes, and realize how much hung upon every word he spoke.

"My child," he said, bending over her, "before I administer the Sacrament that supposes charity with all the world, let me ask you : Could you forgive a great wrong done against yourself by any other? I know you have forgiven freely all the offences of which you know, but if you should discover something else, much more unkind and unprovoked than anything you have ever experienced, could you say, as you hope to be forgiven at God's hands, you from your heart forgave and excused it?"

"I don't think I *could* be angry with any one now."

"Then, Louie, I have something to tell you."

A very few moments sufficed to explain the story to her—the Bishop had sent for Adelaide and wrung from her a full confession; and the miserable girl, waiting outside the door at that very time, had begged, he said, in an agony of remorse, to see her for one moment and ask her forgiveness.

"Oh, sir, I do forgive her, I am not angry at all. May Frances bring her in ?"

Before Frances, little peace-making messenger, had returned from her second errand of love, Louie gave the Bishop one grateful look :

"You believed me when no one else did—I am so glad it's all clear now."

But Adelaide was not alone; when she hid her face and turned away in agony from Louie's whispered pardon, there was, if possible, a whiter and more wretched face to take her place.

"Louie, I have been most unjust to you—most unkind. Can you possibly forgive me?"

"Oh, Miss Barlow! it isn't for me to forgive, when more than half the wrong has been on my side—don't talk about that, please—only we can both be sorry that we were not gentler. I had so little time, I wonder I wasted any of it in hating."

"Can I stay?" she asked almost inaudibly as the Bishop turned toward the open Prayer-book lying on the table. She sank into a seat at a little distance, but Adelaide shook her head when some one asked her to remain, and hurried from the room.

The Bishop and Mr. Rogers, in their surplices, stood beside the Communion-table, Julia and Frances by the bed, Mrs. Seward, Miss Emily, Miss Stanton and Miss Barlow at a little distance. First, the rite of Confirmation, then the administration of the Holy Communion; and, all through their lives, there was not one of that narrow circle who ever heard those two offices again without remembering that scene, the peaceful summer evening, the placid river gleaming through the open windows, the white-robed priests within, *his* voice who read the prayers, *her* face for whom the prayers were said.

At first her eyes eagerly and anxiously searched the Bishop's face, were fastened on it with an appealing, terrified look, that made more than one of those who watched her turn away with a sort of pain; but soon a gentler expression succeeded, and then a holy, happy quiet settled on her face—so different from any look they had ever seen there before, as if she had at last indeed found rest unto her soul, as if the snares and sins of her wayward childhood had at last unloosed their bands; but worn out with the long struggle, as the heavy shackles fell off, the tired child had sunk down, freed and happy, but weary and ready to sleep.

So near unto the Lord had all hearts been lifted, that in the hush that followed the last words of the Benediction, there was not a feeling in any one that could have borne the name of sadness. For those few moments, in their clean and prepared hearts, there was reflected a vision of the Heaven of which they were heirs through hope; till the first mist of earth, a breath of care, a cloud of doubt, crept over the mirror, they saw what awaited the new-born saint, they saw what was the real life— what the only death to fear. For those few mo-

ments things took their true colors; they saw them
as we all shall one day see them,

"Looking o'er life's finished story."

The child whose dying breath fluttered fainter
every minute, was not, they saw then, a trembling
wretch torn from life and love and hope, and thrust
into the coldness and terror of the tomb; but a
young immortal, led tenderly and mercifully
through the path that all must tread, made mercifully short; crowned earlier, sooner safe, than
they.

For a few moments; then came a quick gasp, a
low cry of pain, very, very low, but sharp enough
to show what was yet to be gone through. It
called all back to earth from the peace where they
had been resting.

"I am not frightened," she murmured brokenly,
holding fast the hand that soothed her. "I am not
frightened—but—oh—sir, tell me again, help me—
I can't remember—say it for me—'the—the sharpness of death'"——

"When thou hadst overcome the sharpness of
death, thou didst open the Kingdom of Heaven to
all believers.

"Thou sittest at the right hand of God in the
Glory of the Father.

"We believe that thou shalt come to be our Judge. We therefore pray thee help thy servants whom thou hast redeemed with thy precious blood."

Her face relaxed its look of pain as she sunk back upon the pillow. She opened her eyes and whispered faintly as the Bishop bent over her:

"You will tell mother I tried to be brave?"

"Yes, my darling."

"And that—that leaving her was all that was *very* hard. Tell her she mustn't mind—it's only 'a little while'"——

There was a look stealing over her features that he who had watched by so many death-beds could not mistake; and still holding her hand in his, the Bishop knelt again by the bedside, and read the commendatory prayer. Before it was over, the hand in his relaxed its hold, and when he raised his head, he knew that the face before him, with its sweet radiance of peace, had felt the benediction of angelic hands, and that the saved soul, at rest forever, needed his prayers no more.

CHAPTER XVI.

" But not beneath a graven stone,
   To plead for tears with alien eyes ;
A slender cross of wood alone
   Shall say that here a maiden lies
   In peace beneath the peaceful skies."

A STRANGER stood outside the churchyard, leaning against the railing and watching with sternly
controlled and motionless face the long train of
mourners as they passed out of the lower gate. He
was near enough to see the faces of those who
formed the procession, the classmates and companions of the young girl left behind under that
new mound : and at first he turned away as if unable to bear the sight of their youth and health,
when out of all their number, the only one he cared
for had been struck down; but by degrees his
glance was drawn back by sympathy with the grief
they showed—their mourning dresses and mourning faces did not mock his sorrow, but soothed it,
if anything can soothe sorrow so new as his.

He had arrived too late to hear the burial service, or see the sweet young face now shut forever from human sight.   All that was left to him was the empty church and the fresh-heaped mound and the departing mourners.

He had not heard the words that had comforted *them*, the promises that had taken the sting out of their sorrow, the heaven-piercing faith that had shown them the victory in which death is swallowed up, the blessedness of the dead that die in the Lord, the glory of the immortality which this mortal shall put on, the power of that Resurrection and that life, in which, to believe, is to live forever.

But alone that summer evening, in the quiet churchyard, with the dead of yesterday and the dead of long ago at his feet, Col. Ruthven spent the saddest, but perhaps the most profitable hour of his life.   By the grave of the child who to him had been the brightest, freshest, most living thing in all the world, he learned the frailty of the life on which we stake so much, the folly of all happiness that is only of this earth.   The hopes that died with her left a dreary blank in his soul; but it is in such soil that Heaven's graces best take root, and bear most lasting fruit.

Children ! Don't call this a gloomy story, don't close it with a shudder, and put it away with a chill. It is only the telling that is at fault; for how else does life end? And we are wont to be enough in love with *that*, to read it greedily to the last page. It is only the telling that has failed to reconcile you to Louie's winning a heavenly, instead of an earthly crown; the company of angels, in exchange for the coldness and harshness and treachery of human companionship; safety for struggling—certain victory for uncertain combat—eternal peace for fading pleasure. It is only the telling that has failed to show you,

> "How happier far than life the end
> Of souls that infant-like beneath their burden bend"—

how great their triumph who have died in faith—how pure their pleasure who are safe from sin!

The separation? At longest it is but "a little while"—a little sorrow to be made up by the fullness of joy at God's right hand forevermore; a little pain and loneliness to be forgotten in an everlasting happiness, that, perhaps, could have been purchased at no other price.

Rest—safety—benediction—are sweet words to those who have found how unequal and how deadly is the strife with sin; only you, the cross new on your foreheads and in your hearts, too young to know what lies before you, too buoyant to fear it if you knew—only you think the strife is better than inaction—think the combat has a promise of exultation. To you, perhaps, it would seem a dire calamity if death should come between it and you, but you will not always think so. You will learn to see God's mercy in making any struggle a victory, early or late, in crowning any life with immortality and blessedness and honor.

THE END.

1864.

A NEW CATALOGUE OF

BOOKS

ISSUED BY

CARLETON PUBLISHER,

413 Broadway,

NEW YORK.

NEW BOOKS
And New Editions Recently Issued by
CARLETON, PUBLISHER,
(Late RUDD & CARLETON,)
413 BROADWAY, NEW YORK.

N.B.—The Publisher, upon receipt of the price in advance, will send any of the following Books, by mail, postage free, to any part of the United States. This convenient and very safe mode may be adopted when the neighboring Booksellers are not supplied with the desired work. State name and address in full.

Victor Hugo.
LES MISERABLES.—The only unabridged English translation of "the grandest and best Novel ever written." One large octavo vol., paper covers, $1.00, . or cloth bound, $1.50

LES MISERABLES.—A superior edition of the same Novel, in five handsome octavo vols.— "Fantine," "Cosette," "Marius," "St. Denis," and "Valjean." Cloth bound, each vol., $1.00

THE LIFE OF VICTOR HUGO.—Told by a Witness (understood to be an Autobiography). "Charming and interesting as a Novel." . . . One octavo vol., cloth bound, $1.25

By the Author of "Rutledge."
RUTLEDGE.—A very powerful Novel. 12mo. cl. bound, $1.50

THE SUTHERLANDS.— . . . . . . do. $1.50

FRANK WARRINGTON.— . . . . do. $1.50

LOUIE'S LAST TERM AT ST. MARY'S.— do. $1.25

Hand-Books of Good Society.
THE HABITS OF GOOD SOCIETY; with Thoughts, Hints, and Anecdotes, concerning nice points of taste, good manners, and the art of making oneself agreeable. Reprinted from the London Edition. The best and most entertaining work of the kind ever published. . 12mo. cloth bound, $1.50

THE ART OF CONVERSATION.—A book of information, amusement, and instruction, and one that ought to be in the hands of every one who wishes to be an agreeable talker or listener. . . . . 12mo. cloth bound, $1.00

Mrs. Mary J. Holmes' Works.

MARIAN GREY.—A Novel. . . , 12mo. cloth bound, $1.25
'LENA RIVERS.— . . . . . .   do. $1.25
MEADOW BROOK.— . . . . .   do. $1.25
HOMESTEAD ON THE HILLSIDE.— .   do. $1.25
DORA DEANE.— . . . . . .   do. $1.25
COUSIN MAUDE.— . . . . . .   do. $1.25
DARKNESS AND DAYLIGHT.—(In press.)   do. $1.25

Artemus Ward.

HIS BOOK.—An irresistibly funny volume of writings by the immortal American humorist and showman; with plenty of comic illustrations to match. . 12mo. cl. bound, $1.25

Miss Augusta J. Evans.

BEULAH.—A novel of great power and interest.   Cl. bd., $1.50

Richard B. Kimball.

WAS HE SUCCESSFUL?—   A novel. 12mo. cl. bound, $1.50
UNDERCURRENTS.— . . . do.   do. $1.50
SAINT LEGER.— . . . . do.   do. $1.50
ROMANCE OF STUDENT LIFE.— do.   do. $1.25
IN THE TROPICS.—Edited by R. B. Kimball. do. $1.25

Cuthbert Bede.

THE ADVENTURES OF VERDANT GREEN.—A rollicking, humorous novel of student life in an English University; with more than 200 comic illustrations. . 12mo. cl. bd., $1.25

Edmund Kirke.

AMONG THE PINES.—A thrilling picture of life at the South. 12mo., paper covers, 75 cts., . . or cloth bound, $1.00
MY SOUTHERN FRIENDS; OR, LIFE IN DIXIE.—12mo., paper covers, 75 cts., ... or cloth bound, $1.00
WHAT I SAW IN TENNESSEE.—Paper, 75 cts., or cl. bd., $1.00

The Central Park.

THE ORIGIN, PROGRESS, AND DESCRIPTION, OF THE MAGNIFICENT CENTRAL PARK AT NEW YORK.—Beautifully illustrated with more than 50 exquisite photographs of the principal views and objects of interest. One large quarto, sumptuously bound in . . . . Turkey morocco, $25.00

Ernest Renan.

THE LIFE OF JESUS.—Translated from the original French by C. E. Wilbour. . . . . 12mo. cloth bound, $1.50

A. S. Roe's Works.

A LONG LOOK AHEAD.— . . A novel. . 12mo. cloth, $1.25
I'VE BEEN THINKING.— . . do. . . . do. $1.25
TRUE TO THE LAST.— . . do. . . . do. $1.25
THE STAR AND THE CLOUD.— do. . . . do. $1.25
HOW COULD HE HELP IT.— . do. . . . do. $1.25
IKE AND UNLIKE.— . . . . do. . . . do. $1.25
O LOVE AND TO BE LOVED.— do. . . . do. $1.25
TIME AND TIDE.— . . . . do. . . . do. $1.25

Walter Barrett, Clerk.

THE OLD MERCHANTS OF NEW YORK CITY.—Being personal
incidents, interesting sketches, and bits of biography concerning nearly every leading merchant in New York. Two
series, ... 12mo. cloth bound, each, $1.50

Rev. John Cumming, D.D., of London.

THE GREAT TRIBULATION; OR, THINGS COMING ON THE EARTH.—
Two series, ... 12mo. cloth bound, each, $1.00
THE GREAT PREPARATION; REDEMPTION DRAWETH NIGH.—
Two series. . . . . 12mo. cloth bound, each, $1.00
THE GREAT CONSUMMATION; OR, THE WORLD AS IT WILL BE.—
Two series. . . . . 12mo. cloth bound, each, $1.00
TEACH US TO PRAY.—A volume of devotional sermons on the
Lord's Prayer. . . . . . 12mo. cloth bound, $1.00

M. Michelet's Works.

LOVE (L'AMOUR).—Translated from the French. 12m. cl., $1.25
WOMAN (LA FEMME.)—Translated from the French. . . $1.25
THE MORAL HISTORY OF WOMEN.— do. . . $1.25
WOMAN MADE FREE.—From the French of D'Hericourt, $1.25

Novels by Ruffini.

DR. ANTONIO.—A love story of Italy. . 12mo. cloth, $1.50
LAVINIA; OR, THE ITALIAN ARTIST.— . do. $1.50
DEAR EXPERIENCE.—With humorous illustrations. do. $1.25
VINCENZO; OR, SUNKEN ROCKS.—Paper covers. . . $0.75

F. D. Guerrazzi.

BEATRICE CENCI.—A historical novel. Translated from the
Italian; with a portrait of the Cenci, from Guido's famous
picture in Rome . . . . 12mo. cloth bound, $1 50

Fred. S. Cozzens.
THE SPARROWGRASS PAPERS.—A laughable picture of Sparrowgrass's trials in living in the country; with humorous illustrations by Darley.   12mo. cl. bound, ... $1.25

Epes Sargent.
PECULIAR.—A very clever new novel.   .   12mo. cloth, $1.50

Charles Reade.
THE CLOISTER AND THE HEARTH; OR, MAID, WIFE, AND WIDOW.—A magnificent historical novel.   By the Author of "Peg Woffington," etc.   Reade's best work.   Octavo, cl. bd., $1.50

The Orpheus C. Kerr Papers.
A collection of exquisitely satirical and humorous military criticisms.   Two series. .   12mo. cloth bound, each, $1.25

T. S. Arthur's New Works.
LIGHT ON SHADOWED PATHS.—   12m. cl., $1.25
OUT IN THE WORLD.—(In press.)   .   .   .   .   do.

Stephen Massett.
DRIFTING ABOUT.—By "Jeems Pipes," of Pipesville; with many comic illustrations.   .   .   .   .   12mo. cloth, $1.25

Joseph Rodman Drake.
THE CULPRIT FAY.—A faery poem; tinted paper, cloth, 50 cts.

Mother Goose for Grown Folks.
Humorous rhymes for grown people; based upon the famous "Mother Goose Melodies."   Tinted paper, cl. bd., 75 cts.

Hearton Drille.
TACTICS; OR, CUPID IN SHOULDER STRAPS.—A vivacious and witty West Point love story.   .   .   .   12mo. cloth, $1.00

J. C. Jeaffreson.
A BOOK ABOUT DOCTORS.—A humorous and entertaining volume of sketches about famous physicians and surgeons. .   .   .   .   12mo. cloth, $1.50

Jas. H. Hackett.
NOTES AND COMMENTS ON SHAKSPEARE.—By the great American Falstaff; with portrait of the Author. 12mo. cl., $1.5

New Sporting Work.
THE GAME FISH OF THE NORTH.—An entertaining as well as instructive volume.   Illustrated. .   .   12mo. cloth, $1.50

Docsticks' Humorous Works.
DOESTICKS; WHAT HE SAYS.—With comic illusts. 12m. cl., $1.50
PLURIBUSTAIL.— . . . . . do. do. $1.50
THE ELEPHANT CLUB.— . . do. do. $1.50

H. De Balzac's Novels.
CESAR BIROTTEAU.—Translated from the French, 12m. cl., $1.00
PETTY ANNOYANCES OF MARRIED LIFE.— do. do. $1.00
THE ALCHEMIST.— . . . . do. do. $1.00
EUGENIE GRANDET.— . . . . . . do. do. $1.00

D. D. Home (or Hume).
INCIDENTS IN MY LIFE.—By the celebrated spirit medium; with an introduction by Judge Edmonds. 12mo. cl., $1.25

Thomas Bailey Aldrich.
BABIE BELL, AND OTHER POEMS.—Blue and gold binding, $1.00
OUT OF HIS HEAD.—An eccentric romance. 12mo. cl., $1.00

Adam Gurowski.
DIARY.—During the years 1861 to '63, in Washington. Two volumes, each, ... $1.25

Edmund C. Stedman.
ALICE OF MONMOUTH— . 12mo., tinted paper, cloth, $1.00
LYRICS AND IDYLS.— . . . . 75 cts.
THE PRINCE'S BALL.—With humorous illustrations. . 50 cts.

Alexander Von Humboldt.
LIFE AND TRAVELS.—With an introduction by Bayard Taylor. A book for every library. . . 12mo. cloth, $1.50

Richard H. Stoddard.
THE KING'S BELL— 12mo. cloth bound, tinted paper, 75 cts.
THE MORGESONS.—A novel. By Mrs. R. H. Stoddard. $1.00

M. T. Walworth.
LULU.—A novel of life in Washington. . 12mo. cloth, $1.25

Hugh Miller.
A LIFE of the great Geologist and Author. 12mo. clo., $1.50

Miss Dinah Muloch.
A WOMAN'S THOUGHTS ABOUT WOMEN.—A new work by the Author of "John Halifax," etc. . . 12mo. cloth, $1.25

Isaac Taylor.
THE SPIRIT OF HEBREW POETRY.—With a biographical introduction by Wm. Adams, D.D., of N. Y. 8vo. cl., $2.50

Miscellaneous Works.

HUSBAND & WIFE; OR, HUMAN DEVELOPMENT.—12mo. cl., $1.25
ROCKFORD.—A novel. By Mrs. L. D. Umsted. do. $1.00
SOUTHWOLD.— do. do. do. $1.00
WANDERINGS OF A BEAUTY.—By Mrs. Edwin James. $1.00
THE YACHTMAN'S PRIMER.—By T. R. Warren. do. 50 cts.
SPREES AND SPLASHES.—By Henry Morford. . do. $1.00
THE U. S. TAX LAW.—"Government Edition.". do. 75 cts
THE PRISONER OF STATE.—By D. A. Mahony. . do. $1.25
THE PARTISAN LEADER.—By Beverly Tucker. . do. $1.25
CHINA AND THE CHINESE.—By W. L. G. Smith. do. $1.00
AROUND THE PYRAMIDS.—By Gen. Aaron Ward. do. $1.25
TREATISE ON DEAFNESS.—By E. B. Lighthill, M.D. do. $1.00
THE FLYING DUTCHMAN.—By John G. Saxe. . . do. 50 cts.
NATIONAL CHESS BOOK.—By D. W. Fiske. . . do. $1.50
GARRET VAN HORN.—By J. S. Sauzade. . . . do. $1.25
TWENTY YEARS AROUND THE WORLD. J. G. Vassar. 8vo. $3.50
NATIONAL HYMNS.—By Richard Grant White. 8vo. $1.00
FORT LAFAYETTE.—By Benjamin Wood. 12mo. cloth, $1.00
ALFIO BALZANI.—By Domenico Minnelli. . . do. $1.25
THE NATIONAL SCHOOL FOR THE SOLDIER.— . do. 50 cts.
ORIENTAL HAREMS.—Translated from the French. do. $1.25
LOLA MONTEZ.—Her life and lectures. . . . do. $1.50
ESSAYS.—By George Brimley. . . . . . . do. $1.25
GEN. NATHANIEL LYON.—A life. . . . . do. $1.00
PHILIP THAXTER.—A novel. . . . . . . do. $1.00
FROM HAYING TIME TO HOPPING.—A novel. . do. $1.00
JOHN DOE AND RICHARD ROE.—By E. S. Gould. do. $1.00
MARRIED OFF.—An illustrated poem. . . . . do. 50 cts.
ROUMANIA—By Dr. Jas. O. Noyes. . . . do. $1.50
HUSBAND vs. WIFE.—A poem illustrated. . . . do. 50 cts
BROWN'S CARPENTER'S ASSISTANT.— 4to. $5.00
TRANSITION.—Edited by Rev. H. S. Carpenter. 12mo. cl., $1.00
DEBT AND GRACE.—By Rev. C. F. Hudson. . . do. $1.25
THE VAGABOND.—By Adam Badeau. . . . . do. $1.00
COSMOGONY.—By Thos. A. Davies. 8vo. $1.50
ANSWER TO HUGH MILLER.—By T. A. Davies. 12mo., $1.25
EDGAR POE AND HIS CRITICS.—By Mrs. Whitman. do. 75 cts.
HARTLEY NORMAN.—A novel. . . . . do. $1.25